Jessica Treadway

ABSENT
WITHOUT
LEAVE
AND OTHER STORIES

ABSENT
WITHOUT
LEAVE
AND OTHER STORIES

JESSICA
TREADWAY

delphinium books

harrison, new york   encino, california

Library of Congress Cataloging-in-Publication Data
Treadway, Jessica, 1961–
    Absent without leave and other stories / Jessica
Treadway.—1st
ed.
        p.   cm.
        ISBN 0-671-79213-X : $20.00
        I. Title.
    PS3570.R3576A64   1992
    813'.54—dc20   92-14896
                                    FEB   8 1993   CIP

First Edition   All rights reserved
10 9 8 7 6 5 4 3 2 1

Published by Delphinium Books, Inc.
    P.O. Box 703
    Harrison, NY 10528

Distributed by Simon & Schuster
Printed in the United States of America

Jacket art by Lisa Falkenstern
Text and jacket design by Milton Charles
Production services by Blaze International Productions, Inc.

The following stories appeared in slightly different form in
these publications:
"And Give You Peace" in *The Hudson Review*, Autumn 1984.
"Outside" in *The Atlantic*, April 1990.
"Absent Without Leave" in *Agni Review*, Spring 1992.
"Welcome to Our Village" (originally titled "Frozen") in *The
    Hudson Review*, Autumn 1986.

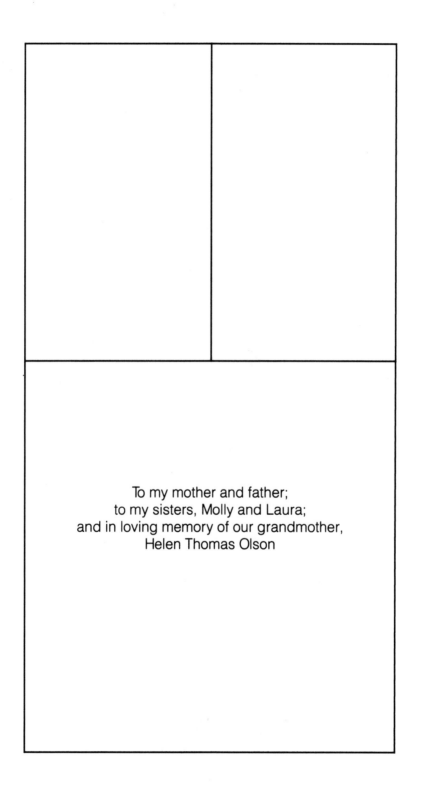

To my mother and father;
to my sisters, Molly and Laura;
and in loving memory of our grandmother,
Helen Thomas Olson

ACKNOWLEDGMENTS

My deepest thanks to Andre Dubus and the Thursday-Nighters, Michael Curtis, Richard Parks, Glenn Pike, Karen Feldscher, Alexandra Broyard, Eileen Kern, and many others known to themselves and me, for whose friendship and support I am grateful beyond words.

Children of the future Age,
Reading this indignant page:
Know that in a former time,
Love! sweet Love! was thought a crime.

William Blake
"A Little Girl Lost,"
Songs of Experience

CONTENTS

**ABSENT
WITHOUT
LEAVE**
AND OTHER STORIES

**AND
GIVE
YOU
PEACE**

AND
GIVE
YOU
PEACE

When the waitress comes, my sister asks her if they serve hamburgers in this restaurant.

"Well, we have the sirloin platter. Number Five," the waitress says, leaning over to point at the menu.

"What is that, basically?" Christine asks.

"A hamburger."

Christine looks at me from under her bangs, and I can see her eyelids rise. "I guess I'll give that a try, then," she says to the waitress, whose badge tells us her name is Nora.

I order the lasagna and settle back in the dark red plastic of the booth we've chosen, close to the window, with a view of a squat Manufacturers Hanover branch across the street and Antonelli's Pizza on the corner. This is the town we grew up in, and nothing has changed since we moved out. Before our father and youngest sister died, the four of us used to order take-out from Antonelli's about once a week, because our mother had left and taken the family's cooking skill with her. Now Christine and I have not been to Antonelli's for months. And I don't know about her, but I never even eat pizza anymore. The smell of the sauce is a physical memory—reminds me always, with a quick nauseous thump, of those nights we spent hunched around the TV, eating slices straight out of the carton while we watched reruns of "I Love Lucy" and "Get Smart," which was our father's favorite. He always used to get red stuff on his chin, laughing at Max when he dialed the phone in his shoe.

"It'll be a year, soon," Christine says casually, letting the ice in her water glass chink against her teeth. She's right; and I guess I had been thinking about it, but not in the front of my mind, where things can hurt if you let them press for too long. I reach for a breadstick and rip off the cellophane with a crackle, then split it and hand over half to my sister. "Thanks," she says, and white crumbs fall down the front of her blouse.

I pick up my fork and make little stabbing taps on the tablecloth. "I wish she'd hurry up with the food," I say, even though I know that if Nora actually appeared at that moment with our orders, it would be hard for me to swallow.

This is the way they died: our father went into Meggy's bedroom on a drizzly July morning, and shot her in the back of the head with a gun none of us had ever seen before. Then (all of this came from the police report afterward, when they had talked to Mr. Hausler next door) Dad walked around the house for a while and then went outside to trim the rosebushes; but after he trimmed them he cut the roses off, too. Then he went back into his own bedroom and shot himself, putting the barrel of the gun to his head. Nobody heard anything, no gunshots, no screams, no bodies falling. Christine found our father when she got home from a party that night, and the police found Meggy when they came a few minutes later.

It wasn't until the next day that the police gave us the letter, which began: "By the time you read this, Meggy and I will be in a better place . . ." The woman on the TV news said the letter was blood-spattered, but actually it was very clean, considering, with only a light trace of something reddish and pale on the top corner. It was folded neatly, and originally it had been addressed to Liz-Christine-Meggy, but then the *Meggy* had been crossed out and the sentence about the two of them being in a better place had been scribbled at the top of the letter. I don't know where it is now. I suppose our mother got rid of it after the funeral, or the police have it somewhere as evidence.

"How much do you think about it, now?" Christine asks me. She is fiddling with the cellophane the breadstick came in.

I shrug and feel I should lie, but I don't. "A lot," I tell her. "You know? All the time."

She nods and looks down at the table, and a brown curl falls across her eyes. Always, before, she would be doing something with her hair as she spoke—twisting it around a finger, sucking on a braid, tucking side pieces behind her ear—but now she just lets it hang there, as if the effort to push it aside is not worth the trouble. "I know what you mean," she says, letting her voice slide low. "Sometimes I can go a whole day without remembering, like when I'm at school and there's stuff going on, a lot of people around and we're all having a good time. I can tell jokes and watch TV and write a paper, and if somebody else wants to talk about something—like this girl Tracey in the next suite, who broke up with her boyfriend over Christmas—I can sit there and listen, and I won't start to cry even if they're losing it all over the place.

"But when it comes time to go to sleep, I wish . . . God had never invented the nighttime. I lie there and begin to feel myself letting go, and then right when I think I'm about to fall off, it comes rushing back at me. Like there's somebody standing over me with a hose, just waiting to blast me with cold water as soon as I start to forget." She balls up the cellophane and drops it in the ashtray. It begins to crinkle back open to its original shape, and she picks it up again with a sighed grunt and stuffs it out of sight in the napkin dispenser at the side of the table.

"I can't stand all this crap in my way," she says.

Now Nora brings me my salad, plunking the small wooden bowl on top of the breadstick crumbs dotting the tablecloth. "Don't I get one, too?" Christine asks, seeing there is no other salad on Nora's tray.

"Only with pasta," Nora tells her. "Otherwise, it's extra."

"Well, I think that *sucks*," Christine says loudly. I am amazed; my sister has always been softspoken, and modest in her language. "I just think it sucks that I can't get a goddam salad with my dinner," Christine continues. Nora looks embarrassed.

"Bring her one and we'll pay the extra," I say under my breath, as if Christine is a child we have to humor to avoid a scene. Nora starts to move away, scribbling on her pad, until Christine calls her back.

"Never mind," she says. "I'll just take some of hers." She leans over to pick out the carrot and radish pieces in my bowl, because she knows I don't like them and she does. "This is something you can only do with a sister," she says to me, smiling, and in that instant it hurts to love so hard.

She's probably just nervous, I tell myself, being back here, and remembering. It was my mother's idea that I should try to talk to Christine, although it was my idea that we come here to do it. Mom is worried about her, says there's something not right about the way she looks, or the way she has been acting. "I don't think she's told anyone at school about what happened," Mom told me. "I just don't think it's healthy." It's true that Christine does not look all that well—she's lost weight, and her face, even in the mornings, is drawn and weary. There is something forced in her voice when she speaks, and she smiles mechanically, without mirth. It occurs to me that she might need to laugh a little.

"Mark told me some jokes the other day," I announce hopefully. "Wait—let me think of how they go." I press my fingers to my forehead and try to retrieve the punchlines.

Mark is my lover. He started out being just a good friend, the brother of a girl I roomed with at school before moving off campus this past semester, with money I got when our father died. Last summer, when it happened, Mark and I were working together in the bookstore on campus when the police called and said there was an emergency. Mark drove me home, getting there in three hours when it normally takes four, and he stayed in town for two weeks after the funeral; I knew he was there even though I did not want to see him. We became lovers one weekend in the fall, after school had started up again. The first part of the weekend I spent crying and punching him and throwing up in the wastebasket, but by Sunday I was letting him close his arms around me, and then I was giving more to him than I had thought it possible for me to give, and losing myself so thankfully in something larger than grief that I ended up crying again, and then we fell asleep crying together.

"What did Grace Kelly have that Natalie Wood didn't?" I ask Christine now, grateful that the jokes have come back to me, because I promised them.

"I give up," she says, dutifully.

"A good stroke. Why didn't Natalie Wood take a bath on the yacht the night she drowned?"

"Oh, God!" Christine says. "I don't know."

"She preferred to wash up on shore."

Christine groans and snickers simultaneously, exposing her teeth in a wide appreciative yawn. I had forgotten how much I missed her. This is the first time we have been together, without other people around, since we went to visit the graves over Easter break. Usually, when we are at our mother's house on the other side of the state (the house we grew up in, here, was finally sold eight months after they carried the bodies out), Mom is always flitting around, asking us if we need anything, not letting us out of her sight, as if she is afraid of what we might do while she is not looking. If she has to go to the store or the dentist or something, she tries to make sure her husband will be around to keep an eye on us. Paul is a little man with a quiet voice, and I don't know how he could stop Christine or me if we got it in our minds to do anything, but for the most part we keep to ourselves and let them both believe they are protecting us. We never talk about the shootings, and if the subject ever threatens to come up—like a finger pressing gently, testing an exposed wound—one of us always manages, at the last minute, to snatch the conversation back safely to the weather or the merits of Mom's Hungarian goulash.

Across from me, Christine has caught her breath sharply and is craning her neck to see out the window. "There's Candy Anderson," she says, softly, pointing through the glass at a stocky girl walking down the street, her plastic clogs flopping on the sidewalk. Candy was a friend of Christine's in high school—could it have been only a year ago, last June, that they stood next to each other on the gym risers at their graduation, singing "The Lord Bless You and Keep You" with the rest of the choir? Like most time recalled with regret, it seems impossible. Do you know that hymn? The words move across the music with a sharp, sweet pain, which, once you've felt it, stays as memory in your bones:

> The Lord bless you and keep you,
> The Lord lift his countenance upon you,
> And give you peace
> And give you peace
> The Lord make his face to shine upon you,
> And give you peace.

We watch as Candy stops to read the menu posted outside Antonelli's, counts the money in her pocket, and goes inside. When the screen door shuts behind her like a slap, we can't see her anymore.

"Don't you want to catch her when she comes out? Just to say hello?" I ask.

Christine twists back around in her seat and sighs. "No," she says. "I thought I would, for a minute, but I changed my mind." She pushes her lips together as if deciding she will not speak again, but then reconsiders and adds, "I don't want to scare her away."

Meggy was a softball player. She played on the team sponsored by Rodney's Refuse Service for three years running, fielding at third base the first year, then moving up to pitcher when she was thirteen and fourteen. We all used to go to her games at the park, after supper on summer nights; I mean, Christine and I went together, and our father would come if our mother wasn't going to be there with Paul. They sort of worked it out by tacit alternation—our father would come on weeknights, and our mother would come to the Saturday morning games. It took her longer to get there, because she lived that much farther away.

Last year, the year she died, Meggy decided she didn't want to play anymore. She told our father it was because she wanted to spend her summer evenings at the park pool, but he didn't believe her and kept bugging her until he made her cry, and then she said, "Okay, okay, if you really want to know, I can't stand going to games knowing you and Mom are afraid you'll see each other, it makes me sick that you can't even look at each other, it makes me want to puke." Then she threw her laundry-battered Rodney's Refuse cap at him in a little fit of drama, and went outside to sit on the swings.

Later, she told Christine and me, she overheard our parents talking on the phone; our father was nearly in tears, saying the divorce had been too much for her, Meggy, to handle. "But *he's* the one who can't handle it," she told us, in the room she shared with Christine, with the door closed and the radio turned up loud. "I can deal just fine."

"Remember Meggy's softball uniform?" I say to Christine. The food has come and Nora sets it down in front of us, moving cautiously as if she's afraid Christine will bite her hand off. Steam rises from my plate and films my sister's startled face, and I realize we have not said Meggy's name out loud, to each other, in nearly a year.

But she seems relieved that I have brought it up. "The way she washed her jersey so many times, so the letters would fade out?" she says. Meggy had always been embarrassed to wear RODNEY'S REFUSE across her chest. "She always wanted to play for The Golden Fox, remember?" It was a restaurant in the city.

"Yeah." I bite into my lasagna and chew it quickly.

"Remember whenever we played Crazy Eights, the loser had to smell the winner's feet?"

"Of *course* I remember—I broke a blood vessel in my nose when she beat me that time."

"And the night she swallowed all the cough medicine by accident."

Christine snickers. "She was drunk as a skunk. She kept rolling off the sofa and cracking herself up."

"Yeah, I remember." I take a sip of milk, and then I have to smile. "Look at us. Talking about Meggy. Dr. Nettelson should be here to listen to us now."

Christine's face darkens. "I never liked that woman," she says, reaching for the Heinz.

Dr. Nettelson was the shrink our mother made us go to last summer, beginning a week after the funeral. Mom herself had to see the doctor, but that was in the hospital, where they took her for two weeks after she got hysterical at the church service—she started screaming and crying and calling out Meggy's name, and she threw her handkerchief at our father's coffin but it fell before it touched the wood, so she started taking her clothes off and throwing *them*, before Paul and Uncle John grabbed her and took her outside.

Dr. Nettelson was on call that day and admitted our mother to the psychiatric wing of the hospital, where they saw each other two times a day during our mother's stay. Christine and I went less often, twice a week to Dr. Nettelson's office, sometimes together and sometimes separately. She was always comparing us to things: when we couldn't say much to her (because it was so fresh and we did not want to give it away), she said our anger was like rice boiling over a pot on the stove, spilling down the edges with nothing to catch it up. That one killed me. She just wasn't someone I felt like trusting, personally, but I did not hate her the way Christine did. I remember her asking the doctor if she didn't think oatmeal would make a better emotional metaphor, because it was so much messier than rice when it stuck onto something, so much harder to clean up.

"I didn't like her much, either," I say to Christine. She nods approval, shreds of lettuce peeking out of her mouth. "But Teen—there *were* a couple of things that came up, when I talked to her, that I always meant to ask you about . . . but I just didn't."

She looks at me suspiciously—maybe fearfully is a better word—and stops eating. "Like what?"

"Well, for one, I always wondered if you blamed me for not being there," I say. "When it happened? I mean, my deciding to stay on campus last summer and work? You pretty much had to take care of Meggy, and the house and everything, by yourself."

She makes a face and tilts her water glass back, catching the last sliver of ice to crunch between her teeth. "It's okay," she says. "If I could have gone away somewhere, I would have, too."

"It didn't have anything to do with you or Meggy, why I didn't come back," I tell her. "It was all just Mom and Dad."

"Oh, I know," she says, nodding. "I—you know."

"Okay," I say. For a few minutes we eat in silence, looking at our food. It could end here, but there is something else I want to ask, something I need to know to fill a blank space, a space now filled with a furious red terror in my dreams at night. Actually I am afraid to hear the answer, but I ask anyway.

"What did it look like? When you found Dad?" I say. "I mean—just what did it look like?"

Her mouth drops slightly, and she pushes her lips hard into the napkin in her fist. For a moment I am afraid she may run from the booth, because the table gives a quick tremble under her hands as she brings them away, slowly, from her face. But then she is still again, and her fingers, when she grips her fork, are calm.

"I can't talk about that, Liz," she says, and her voice is a combination of apology and horror. "Just please don't ask me again, ever, okay?" She looks down at her plate, where half of the burger and most of the fries float in a ketchup pool. "Do you think the waitress will mind all this mess?"

But no, as it turns out, Nora doesn't mind, in fact is probably very glad to escape unassaulted by Christine, as she whisks all the dishes from the table with a flourish, letting silverware clatter on the tray as it falls. Christine and I both move to take out our wallets, but I make her put hers back. "At least let me leave the tip," she says, and tucks four dollar bills under the empty water glass. When she sees my surprised look she defends herself: "Why not? I mean, for putting up with *me*."

In the restroom she uses the stall first while I look in the mirror and knead the skin around my eyes, which look old and tired, even though I don't feel either of those things today. I look closer to thirty, instead of twenty, and this is curious because Christine has changed in exactly the opposite way: she seems to have lost age in her face and taken on a deliberate, safe innocence, like Meggy's.

"Liz?" Christine says to me. I wait; behind the stall she is crying, the short choppy cry of a just-punished child. "Don't come in," she tells me, as I put my hand on the door.

"What, then?" I say, alarmed.

"I just want to ask you what you think," she says, and her nose is stuffing up. "Do you think he would have killed me, too, if I hadn't gone up to the lake for the party? They said he didn't shoot himself right away, after Meggy. Do you think he was waiting for me?" Just saying this seems to scare her, and her voice rises high on a choked breath.

It is probably not smart, I think, to let her know I have wondered about this myself. "No, Teen," I say, and hope I sound convincing. "I think what he said in the letter was true—he thought you and I could handle it, his—dying. But Meggy . . . well, you know how he always felt about her." I pause before adding, "And I think Dr. Nettelson was right when she said he just kind of snapped at the end, and nobody could have guessed what he was thinking." This seems to help. I can hear her blowing her nose into toilet paper, and the crying noise has stopped.

"Okay," she says. Her voice is tired, spent, but sounds freer of the dread I've heard in it recently. She takes a deep breath, and a leftover sob escapes in a comical gasp, like a burp. "Oh, pretty noise," she says, and then she laughs, and my heart twists at the sound, which is one of the oldest sounds it knows.

"Listen, about the waitress, and the salad thing," she says. "I just want you to understand. Sometimes I get like that—I get mad at people for no reason, and I blow up, and I can't do anything to help it. You know?" I nod, forgetting she can't see me. "Liz?" she says again.

"Yes," I answer, thinking of Mark, of feeling the breathless punch in my chest slow down when he touches my hand. I want to let Christine know what is out there waiting for her, but what can one person promise another about this? About what starts up, again, when your world has ended?

"Hurry up, Teen," is all I tell her, "I have to pee." This is something you can only do with a sister.

When we come out, two women have taken our booth, and walking toward them I recognize the fat one with a sharp stutter of breath. She is Mrs. Sparkman, who used to work with our mother in the library at the elementary school. It's too late to pass her by, because she has recognized us, too, and her eyes are briefly startled, then filled with thrill and pity. "Well, *hello*," she says, catching my eye, calling us over to the table with a wave. "How are you, girls? This is my sister-in-law, Phyllis Sparkman. Phyllis, meet Liz and Christine Burnside." She pauses for breath and surveys us curiously. "How *are* you, girls?" she repeats.

"Burnside?" The sister-in-law is tapping her fingers on her forehead, scrunching up her face. "Why do I know that name, Lydia?"

"You don't," Mrs. Sparkman tells her abruptly. A sudden spastic move of her body makes me believe she has tried to kick the other woman under the table.

"But I could *swear* . . ." the sister-in-law says, clearly frustrated.

"Don't knock yourself out," Christine says. "Our father killed our little sister last year, and then he killed himself, and it was all over the papers and TV, so that's probably how you know our name. Yes, that was us," she continues, as the woman looks up at Christine with a horrified look on her face. "By the way, that necklace you're wearing is so adorable I could just puke." It is a thick gold chain supporting a round blue bead, with a bouquet of pink buds painted in the middle. Meggy had barrettes just like it. Christine says all of this very calmly and turns to leave, and I follow her outside, as if this were a normal thing that just happened, as if she had just told the women she was majoring in English and they should try the sirloin platter.

"That wasn't the right thing to say," she acknowledges, when we are out on the sidewalk in the hot gray haze of the June twilight. "I know that. I know it. Liz, do you think there's something wrong with me?" She stands on the corner with her hands thrust deep inside her jeans pockets, letting her hair hang into her worried eyes.

"No," I tell her, though I cannot explain why. Just: "No."

"Okay," she says. There is a pause. "Look, I would never to back to Dr. Oatmeal," she tells me, "but there *is* this guy at school, he works in counseling, who this girl Tracey sees. I might stop over and introduce myself, when classes start again."

"That's a good idea, Teen," I say, trying to sound casual, so as not to let her know what a really good idea I believe it is.

"Well, I'm *thinking* about it," she says. We are about to move toward the car when we see a line of kids on bikes whizzing up the street toward the park, riding no-handed, with bright towels rolled up and tucked under their armpits. The park pool must have just opened for the season. The kids are young, Meggy's age, some of them Meggy's friends, both boys and girls, who came to the funeral as a group and left soggy wads of Kleenex in the pew. I recognize a few of them as they ride by, shouting to each other over the whirr of many pedals: "I call the first dive!" "You don't even know how to dive, pansy-ass." "Is Ronnie meeting us there, or are we picking her up?"

Christine and I look down at the sidewalk as they pass by, and I know both of us are thinking about Meggy's blue bike, a present from our parents on her twelfth birthday. After Meggy died our mother gave the bike to Sybil Tierney down the street, on the condition that Sybil wouldn't roll the odometer back to zero, but save the miles Meggy had left there.

"Remember how that used to be the most important thing?" Christine says, when the kids are out of sight. "Going to the pool after dinner in the summer? Remember how Jeb at the snack bar used to give us free Nutty Buddies? Oh, God—I actually remember telling Dad I was going to *kill* myself, if he didn't let me go that time."

"But he did," I say, finishing the story. Across the street, somebody in Antonelli's flips on the red neon PIZZA-BEER light above the window. Our eyes snap to the familiar sign like fireflies to a lamp. "You don't feel like getting a pizza, do you?" I ask, and my sister looks at me with surprise for an instant before she knows I am only kidding. For the first time in a long time she really smiles, meaning it, relaxing the tight, about-to-vomit grimace at the corners of her mouth.

"No," she says, resting a palm on her stomach, then reaching up to shove her hair out of her eyes. In front of the dingy sun she looks as if she might dare to believe, again, that this is the best place and time to be. "I've had enough, for now."

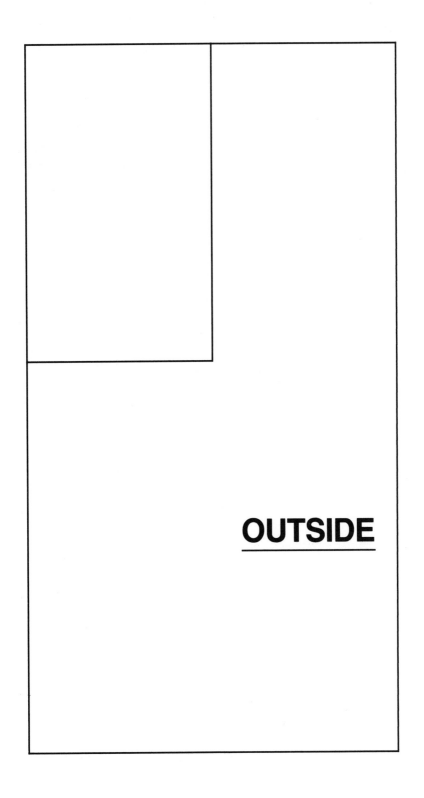

OUTSIDE

OUTSIDE

They were all sitting in the backyard when Joe Wheeler walked by.

"Don't look now," Ruthie murmured, into her *Mademoiselle*. "On the waterline."

They all looked out across the lawn. He had on shorts, a T-shirt, and a white hat with the brim pulled down close around his face. There was a white towel bunched at the back of his neck. Even from this distance, they could see sweat sliding down his legs.

"He looks just like he did when he used to play tennis." Susan lifted her sunglasses, then pulled them down again discreetly when it seemed Joe Wheeler might be turning her way. But instead he moved ahead slowly, on stiff knees.

"He's a lot thinner, though. God, he looks like an old man." Their mother kept watching until he was out of sight, across the street and farther down the long dirt path covering the water-supply route from the reservoir into town. Between the rows of black raspberries, people ran and rode bicycles in the hottest part of the day.

"Who is he?" Susan's husband wanted to know. Every time he slapped at the mosquitoes lighting on his legs, he missed. The women were laughing at him with their eyes.

"Joe Wheeler." Ruthie spoke to the pages of the magazine, which was open to an update on penile implants. She held it tilted at an angle so her mother wouldn't see. "We used to babysit for them—his kids, I mean. But one summer they just stopped calling." She closed the magazine around her finger and turned her gaze across the grass. "I wonder why that was."

"It was a long time ago," Susan said.

"But what's the matter with him?" Her husband pointed at the waterline with his beer can. It was the Fourth of July, and they were waiting for night. Already, early fireworks sounded from other parts of the town, muted blasts and pops that made them imagine there was a war being fought at some distant front.

"Cancer," the women's mother said. "Last summer he went to the doctor because he thought he'd strained his back on the tennis court. Turned out he had a tumor on his spine, and they gave him a month, at first. Can you imagine? Going in to the doctor for a pulled muscle, and coming out with a month to live?" She clapped vigorously in the air, and when she separated her palms, flakes of mosquito stuck to her skin. The rest of them looked away.

"But he responded to the chemo," she continued, smoothing lotion across her chest. "He's been hanging on for a year now. I saw Caroline at the 7-Eleven the other day, and she said they're planning to bring their girl—Penny, is that her name?—up to Vermont at the end of August. Joe takes pain pills, she said. Long car rides aren't the greatest, but it sounds like that's his big goal. Get his daughter to college, then come home to die."

"Yuck," Ruthie said. She shivered under the sun.

" 'Course, that's not how Caroline put it," her mother said. "That's just my take of the clues."

Susan had pulled off her glasses and was sucking on one of the ends. She looked hard at her husband, who was licking Dorito dust from his fingers, until he noticed and looked back at her.

"What?" he said.

"I'm just trying to figure out what it would feel like," Susan told him. "Knowing you were going to die. Not knowing when, but watching you get sicker. Weak, like that. Skinny. Like an old man, waiting not to wake up one day." For a moment her intensity made them all hold their breath. Then she put the glasses on and leaned back in her chaise, and the strain of concentrating left her face, as if she'd made a decision that relieved her. "No," she said, adjusting her body to get comfortable across the plastic weave. "No way could I handle that."

Her husband was squinting, though a cloud passed overhead. "Well, I'll do my best," he told Susan. "Jeez."

In the house, the phone rang. "Dad'll get it," their mother said. A few minutes later, Susan and Ruthie's father came out to the yard and stood at the edge of the circle their lawn chairs made by the grill.

"The sun, Dad," Ruthie said, and he stepped back to draw his shadow away from her face.

"Weird phone call," he told them, squatting down in the grass. "It was a tape from the town police. Saying a kid from over on Pearl Road is missing, named Steven Lang. Dressed in shorts and a Florida T-shirt, red high-tops, six years old. They must be dialing up all the numbers for a couple of streets square, so people can keep out an eye."

"Hey, like those advertising tapes," Susan said. "Where you come home at the end of the day, and you think you have all these messages because the machine takes so long to rewind, and when you play it all you get is a damn robot talking about some time-share out on the Cape."

"I never heard of the police doing it, though." Her mother shaded her eyes and gave a long peer out across the yard, in case she might spot the missing child picking raspberries. "What a great idea. I hope he's okay." She looked beyond her husband's shoulder until a wasp flittered near her hair. When she was finished swatting she tapped her husband's hand, so he would know she was talking to him, and said, "We're waiting for Joe Wheeler to come back down the line."

He rubbed his eyebrows and stared ahead into his memory. "Hey, whatever happened to them?" he asked his daughters. "One of you used to be over there every Saturday night."

Susan spit back into her glass an ice cube that turned out to be too big. "I guess we fell out of touch," she said.

Joe Wheeler was amazed at the world. With every step he could smell the dry dirt his shoe displaced and sent spreading into the air. He tried by stopping suddenly, a few times, to locate the exact point at which the particles became invisible as they rose from his feet; but they dissolved slyly against his blond shins, as if beating him at a race.

As he moved forward on the path, he was aware of the bugs flying around his face, but it seemed that by the time he got his hand up to shoo them, they had either bitten him or flown ahead. The green around him, and the brown under his heels, were sharp one moment and indistinct, flickery, the next. Dying, or at least his dying, was like that: like driving a car over a hill road, losing the radio signal in the high rock. The way a song came clear at the crest, then passed in and out of static as the car moved up and down through the gray: it was like that. Except that a radio could be fiddled with, turned up in volume, or switched off. Joe had no controls. And when his senses were working, they often came in too strong—he heard things people meant to be secret, or saw details no one else could discern.

He walked slowly, because his legs were sore at the hips, and because he was afraid that if he moved too fast he wouldn't notice something he couldn't afford to miss, like a car coming down one of the crossroads, or a kid speeding by on a bike. Three people passed him on the waterline, two women and a man; the women did not even look up, and the man turned his face to spit on the other side of the bushes as Joe hurried to get out of his way.

He stopped again by a thick-berried branch. Was he invisible? He ate some of the berries straight off the leaves—no point in waiting to wash them, that was a plus. They tasted dusty until he bit in, but the juice was sweeter this way. He was proud of the care he took to save himself from the thorns.

He turned to watch the joggers receding, their bodies bobbing toward Fairview Drive. He could not believe that they hadn't seen him, but silent intersections didn't surprise him anymore. A year ago, if he had passed the same man going at the same speed, they would have raised their hands above their heads in a high slap as their courses crossed. Now people moved by him without acknowledging he was there. It was as if they didn't trust him, because he knew something they could not.

It happened, sometimes, even at home—the other night his daughter came into the living room to turn on the TV, and Joe, waking from a nap, had to speak up before being sat on. The rest of the family laughed when he told them about it, but Penny's eyes had turned nervous since then. And his son, Matt, trying to escape admitting what it summoned in all of them, poked Penny and said, "It's not like he's history *yet*," and then Joe saw in Matt's face the most damaging kind of regret, and shock at the arrow he had shot from his own tongue. The wound to Joe's soul was not as deep as what he felt for Matt at the same moment— forgiveness, and the knowledge that he would be gone long before Matt ever understood it had been granted. That was what being a father meant, living or dead, and he knew this if nothing else would survive the subversion of his flesh.

Before he left on his walk today, he felt the waiting in Caroline, too. She was sitting in the kitchen, eating ice cream and reading a book. "Why don't you take that outside?" he suggested. "It's too nice to be wasting the sun." She didn't answer, but he could sense guilty irritation in her sigh. And he knew what she was thinking, the truth she would never have said out loud, but which they both heard in her silence: *I don't have to hoard anything.* When he left, Penny and Matt were fighting over the remote control buttons to the TV.

He moved away from the bushes and came in a few steps to the brook that crossed the waterline before Pearl Road. Every time he approached the brook, and passed above it, he listened to the water rushing over rocks. Even on winter days, when the ground was frozen and the water's path was softened, narrowed by snow, there was always the small sound of movement, a wordless whisper he could hear if he stopped walking and there was no interference from wind. Today the sound was louder than usual, because there was something else in the brook besides stone and silt, causing the flow to rise and splash over its square gray bulk.

It was a refrigerator in the stream.

Someone had rolled it end over end down the shallow bank; behind it, through the trees, he could see the trail of drag marks through a backyard on Herber Avenue. The freezer section was open, its handle stuck in the mud. But the refrigerator itself was closed, and a sucking noise ran through the rubber lip. WHIRLPOOL shimmered in silver at the surface.

Joe took a slippery step off the waterline, into the grass, and grabbed a raspberry branch by accident as he lost his foothold. Thorns stabbed at his palms and he swore, stumbling. Then his skin turned cold, not from the wetness in his shoes but at the sight of a piece of cloth, the end of a small shirttail, trapped inside the door. On the other side of the refrigerator, he saw now, a child's bicycle lay against the stream bank, its spokes revolving lazily under the humid breeze.

Joe pitched himself on top of the door and pulled at the handle, trying to find some leverage on the wet rocks, but his shoes gave up their grip and he slid down into the stream. The sucking sound increased along the rubber seal. The door sat high, at an angle away from him, and he had to reach across the slick flank to press upward with the useless muscles at the underside of his arms. They felt like twine, not taut but twangy, and his legs ached from being twisted by a body too weak for its weight. As he pressed, his eyes lifted to ground level, where he envisioned shoes passing, pausing, and plunging in to offer their help, but it was only a vision; no one walked by.

Where were the joggers? Why weren't the ones who had ignored him, going one way, coming back on their return leg? And another question, pounding in his temples while the sweat itched and stabbed at the inside of his lids: why hadn't they seen, as they went by the water, the refrigerator, the bicycle, the fabric wedged in the giant door?

The sky above him was silent, and dust lay on the waterline, waiting to be disturbed. But no one approached it. He was alone with water and death. He kicked at the door hinge, heaved again at the handle, shouted, and felt it give. His final strength pried it open; he crawled up and flattened his body against it, so it couldn't swing shut again.

Then the breath he took stalled in his chest when he saw the boy.

He had fallen with the dislodging of the door to the refrigerator's back wall, his head curled forward and his fingers tucked under his chin. The chamber smelled sour, like bad milk, and Joe felt a gagging noise rise in his throat as he reached forward to touch the boy. His fingers jumped at contact with the warm skin of the small arms, and he realized he had expected it to be chilled. He pulled the body out and without realizing at first what it was felt the slow heart vibrating beneath the red shirt, which showed an island, blue water, and sand.

The boy's head fell limp on his shoulder, and when Joe moved to step out of the brook he slammed the huge door back down toward the refrigerator's body, and the force made him fall to his knees against the wet stones; but still he held the boy. Using his free hand to help himself up the bank, by gripping grass and, then, pushing himself up to sit on the level ground, he laid the boy back, with the island facing the sky. Again, before tilting the head and breathing into the slack red mouth, he looked down the waterline and saw emptiness at both ends. The path stretched ahead green into curves he had memorized but couldn't, from here, see.

He exhaled into the boy, breath and sound he couldn't control, watching the chest rise under his own pale hand.

After a minute the boy's knees rose, bringing his feet in close to his body, and he coughed. Joe held the back of his head up then, and as the boy gasped his cheeks lost their plum flush and his eyes settled into seeing, focusing on Joe's face. He started to cry, until Joe put his hand against the boy's forehead and gave it a gentle press. Joe wanted to smile at him, but caught himself in time; lately, when he smiled at his children, or even at Caroline, they winced in returning it, and when he went to the mirror he understood why. The flesh of his face was like loose wax, shiny over high bones, and his teeth looked dark against the transparency of his lips. But the boy, who was closer than his family came now, didn't seem frightened; and Joe kept his own shadow circling the boy's head until he told Joe he wanted to sit up.

"What happened?" Joe asked him, the words squeezing through his chest. He felt the back of his shorts turning to mud as the water absorbed the dirt they were sitting in. He knew they would have to move on as soon as his breath returned—the boy's skin didn't look right yet, and his chest still made jerky shivers, like a dreaming dog. "What's your name?" Joe said.

The boy hugged himself around the middle. "Steven Theodore Lang," he said quietly, biting into his knee. Then he looked up, and Joe saw confession in his eyes. "I'm not allowed on the waterline, but I heard my mother say there was a dying guy out here sometimes. Me and Eric Koone saw somebody dumping their fridge here last night, and it looked like a good place for a dying guy to hide." He coughed again, and Joe felt the violent shaking in his own lungs.

"So I just came down to look while my mother was at the 7-Eleven, but I couldn't see over the edge. I climbed up and fell on something, and I grabbed the door by accident, and it knocked me inside." Steven's chest puckered in spasm at the memory. The word *mother* had drowned in his throat. "I couldn't push it back open. Everything was black, and nobody could hear me." Then his breath shud-

dered into calm, the fear left his eyes, and the smile he
turned up at Joe was like nothing he had ever seen before
on a child's face, like nothing he had ever felt in his wife's
touch, or dared to look for in the part of himself he had only
come to recognize in the last year. As he leaned forward to
hear the rest of what the boy said, he was aware of a rise
under his ribcage, and he remembered with a shock
stronger than terror that this sensation was called hope.

"Do you want to hear what I was dreaming?"

A chill bit Joe's neck; the towel he had wrapped there at
the start of the walk was sopping with sweat and brook
water, and he felt it slip on his skin.

"Wait here," he said to Steven, before his lust to know
could betray him. He made a pillow of the towel at the edge
of the path. The numbness in his arms told him they
wouldn't bear the boy's weight, and there was no one, no
one, near them.

He walked as fast as his frame would carry him, brushing
by berry branches, breathing in bugs. He strained his eyes
looking for the people who'd passed him earlier, and for
the first time he remembered, like an old geometry theorem
he had learned weakly long ago, that a person traveling in
one direction could reach his original place by making a
circle, instead of returning the way he had come.

When he drew in sight of Fairview Drive he paused,
praying for breath, and before him he could see members
of the Bell family still sitting in their yard. They looked up
briefly at the sound of a skyrocket, but only at each other,
and not beyond. When he passed by them earlier, he
waved but they didn't see him, and he felt silly holding his
hand up in the air waiting for them to notice, so he turned
his eyes back to the path and pretended to study the dirt.

He used to drive Ruthie and Susan Bell back to this
house after babysitting. He remembered the day he came
home after a tennis game at the Gibsons'—Caroline hung
around to help sweep the court—and found one of the
girls, he couldn't remember which, touching herself in the

bathroom. Matt and Penny were playing outside, and Joe assumed that the babysitter was with them. He discovered her suddenly, kicking open the door with a clay-dusted sock, taking his sweaty shirt off over his head as he moved by instinct toward the shower faucet. She was sitting on the toilet seat with her shorts down when he turned and saw her, and she sucked in her breath on a shriek as she jumped up, yanked at her waistband, and stumbled down the stairs and outside, where (he watched her from the second-story window, after recovering from his own fright) she sprinted up the street and around the corner, toward home. A few days later, Caroline told him that the Bell sisters weren't working as babysitters anymore. "She just said something about boyfriends," Caroline said. "I suppose it had to happen sometime."

As he approached their circle, he tried in the instant before he called out to imagine what they would see. One of the girls lay on her stomach, with her hair hanging above a magazine; the other reclined under dark glasses, though the sun was behind the trees. Their mother was losing part of a cheeseburger down the front of her bathing suit, and the two men were trying to tune in the Red Sox more clearly.

Closer, Joe realized it was the girl lying on her back he had surprised seven years ago. He wanted to smile at her, and show that all was forgiven, even funny, in the face of what they fought now. He was opening his mouth to let air in, to tell them what was needed, when he heard her sister mumble over the magazine.

"Don't look now," she said, in a voice he knew she believed was invisible through meat smoke and the sound of explosion in a far sky. "He's coming."

COMMENCEMENT

COMMENCEMENT

My daughter believes she is graduating from high school tonight, but I have information to the contrary. The guidance counselor called me at work around noon—I ended up being late for lunch with Stu Markham—to tell me about a "glitch" in Francie's exam results. The glitch is that she flunked her algebra final, and this leaves her a credit shy of the number she needs to get a diploma. They didn't locate the grading error until today, but when they did, they called immediately, so there would be no confusion about what it means.

"She can make it up in summer school," the guidance counselor said, "but I'm afraid there's nothing she can do in time for the ceremony tonight."

Was there a certain amount of smugness in the guidance counselor's voice as she told me this? Her name is Mrs. Osterhaut, and I remembered that Francie hates her guts, because of something somebody once said about the gym teacher, who had Mrs. Osterhaut place Francie under internal suspension for three days. This means you sit in the guidance center with a bunch of rejects, and pretend to be sorry for what they think you did, Francie explained to her mother and me at the time.

"She has some trouble figuring," I told Mrs. Osterhaut. "She gets that from her old man." I tried to keep things light between us grown-ups, but I must not have tried hard enough, because Mrs. Osterhaut went straight on to say that whatever the problem was, she was sorry but Francie would not be eligible to graduate this evening.

"Look," I said. "I guarantee she'll pass it in summer school. I'll get her a tutor. But you can't just let her not graduate, for God's sake. Couldn't she just march with everyone else, as a formality?"

But Mrs. Osterhaut wasn't listening, or if she was, she didn't give a damn. "Those are the rules," she told me sternly, as if she now understood why Francie Griffith was a discipline problem. "She should sign up for remedial right away, because you don't want something like this hanging over her head," she added, before urging me to have a good one.

I hung up and tried to call my wife, but got no answer. Francie had skipped graduation rehearsal and was up at Lake George with some of her friends. There was nothing I could do with my piece of news except wish I hadn't been there to receive it, so I went to lunch and apologized to Stu for being late. Then I encouraged him to talk about his own children, who are failures in what my kids would call a big way, the son being addicted to pills and the daughter pregnant by what my kids called a total scumbag. I left the restaurant in a beer haze and feeling fine about things, and forgot to try calling Elaine again when I was back in the office.

The afternoon passed quickly. For the first time since I began to dread coming to work in the morning—it's been about fifteen years now—I feel sorry to have to leave. On my way home I stop at the VFW post for a few pops, to settle my stomach. Earl has a cold one waiting for me as I take my stool. "You're early today," Earl says. I explain the situation, and what's on my mind—the impossible thing I have to tell my daughter.

"Honesty's the best policy, Art," one of my friends, Ted, advises me, after I lay out the whole story. Ted's wife calls a few minutes later, and Ted asks Earl to tell her he hasn't so much as popped his head into the post all week. We have a laugh over that, and because his wife called, Ted has to buy a round. When I am about to leave, Earl pours me another one on the house.

"To get your nerve up," Earl says, draining the foam off, so I have to stay for a while.

Before I go home I stop at the Rite Aid to pick up some Certs, and after stalling in the aisles for a few minutes I also buy Francie a blue hairband with a design of flowers across the top. It's an unusual thing for me to do, something I didn't plan. But I suppose I am trying to buy time, more than a gift, and it isn't the hairband I want as much as the sympathy it might convey to Francie, who has been talking about this graduation night since her class began ordering caps and gowns in the spring. As I pull into the driveway it occurs to me that maybe I should feel anger toward her, instead of pity, but this doesn't really seem fair, since I wouldn't know an algebraic solution if it greeted me at breakfast, and daughters should by their nature know less than fathers do.

When I get there Elaine and our other daughter, Jill, are in the kitchen, using M&M's to spell out *Happy Grad Day!* on top of a chocolate cake. "Is that you, Dad?" Jill calls cautiously, as I step inside the door. She is sneaking handfuls of candy from the bag, especially the green ones, which are supposed to make you horny. (Francie told this to all of us over the dinner table recently. I can remember when she used to blush in front of me if someone mentioned the breast stroke.)

"Of course it's me," I say. "Who were you expecting, the Boston Strangler?" But only Jill smiles, and only a little. The two of them look nervous, as if they are the ones who are graduating, and when I go over to give Elaine a kiss hello, she puts her hand up to stop me.

"Don't, Art," she says. "There isn't time," she adds, as if this is the reason she won't let me near. Jill looks away at the floor. "If you want something to eat, you'd better grab it," Elaine adds.

I reach into the refrigerator and take out a can of Bud.

"To *eat*," my wife tells me, so I pick up a beater from the bowl and lick off a chunk of frosting.

"The Griffith Family Guide to Good Nutrition," Jill says, and this time Elaine laughs too.

"Where's Francie?" I ask, ripping open the flimsy bag the drugstore gave me. On top of the sales slip the hairband bobs round and rigid, and I notice it isn't a pattern of flowers stitched onto the fabric, but butterflies with their wings open.

"She's at the hair shrine," my wife informs me, "where else?"

I go up to the girls' bedroom and find Francie sitting in the swivel chair at the vanity mirror, surrounded by the familiar arrangement of cotton balls, brushes, powders, and pins, gripping the handle of the metal rod she uses in daily torture sessions on her hair. She is the better-looking of the girls, with smart dark eyes, clear skin, and a body she inherited from Elaine's side of the family, slender at the waist but tautly curved above it, soft hair swinging down her back. Sometimes when I drop her off at school in the morning and watch the boys come up, I wish she could be a sloucher like her sister. But more often I feel the way I do now, as I stand in the threshold waiting to go in—proud, and hardly able to believe that something so beautiful could contain some of my blood. She wears a white dress and fancy sandals, and she is lifting her eyebrows at her own image in the rouge-smudged glass.

"Hi, hon," I say, and go over to touch her shoulder. The thought of talking with Francie pleases me. We haven't had much to say to each other lately, not since Elaine and I turned down her request for a car as a graduation gift. (We considered the idea briefly, but only because we live in the kind of suburb where not considering it could be construed as child abuse.) In the end we settled on the same thing we gave Jill when she went to college, a set of suitcases. We hid them in our bedroom closet and planned to give them to Francie with the cake, after the family comes home from graduation and before she goes off to all the parties it inspires.

"Hi," Francie says back, and her arm jerks as if allergic when I touch her sleeve with my beer can. She doesn't turn to look up, but I see her eyes follow me above her own reflection. "I wasn't sure you'd make it, Dad," she adds, softly, and I have to lean closer to hear what it is she's saying.

"You weren't? Honey, are you kidding?"

"Well, *you* know," she says, and a sheepish smile comes back at me from the mirror. Then I catch a heady whiff, like the rush of swift gin spreading, as she sprays her wrists and throat from a bottle with a French name and a scent that seals my throat up. "We have to go in a couple minutes," she reminds me, turning brisk, replacing the fragrant lid.

"I know. But France, listen. I have to tell you something."

"Can't it wait?"

"Not really. Listen, I got this phone call today—"

"Dad, can't you just leave me alone!" The noise of her sudden explosion makes me flinch. "Why are you standing there yakking away at me like this? First of all, these moron high heels are killing me. Second of all I'm supposed to be there in eight minutes! Will you please let me finish my hair?" She yanks the hot stick from her bangs with a snarl, and combs the hair down in front of her eyes like a mask, to punctuate her frustration. I think of leaving the new hairband for her to play with, but remember that I might need it later as a kind of consolation prize, so I carry it with me out of the room and back down to the kitchen.

"She's a little hyper," I say to Elaine.

"A *little* hyper." Elaine is putting lipstick on, making faces at the hallway mirror. "Look who's talking, Twitch." The nickname is an old joke between us—so old that when she says it I am startled, and immediately hopeful. She turns to smile at me, but before her lips are all the way up, she pushes them into a tissue. I put my beer down and take a step closer.

"Lainie, listen—" But the moment is over as she picks up the beer bottle and stuffs her tissue through the neck. I catch myself before exclaiming that I haven't finished the beer yet. She waits, impatient, to find out what I want from her at this crucial, distracted time. I go over next to her, and my breath fails. "You missed a spot," I say, reaching up to rub a scrap of clotted lipstick from her mouth.

There does not seem to be any way to tell my family that Francie will not, indeed, be graduating. I try once more, feebly, in the car on the way to the school, but Francie cuts me off with a list of the classmates she wants us to notice during the ceremony, when their names are called. "Jonathan Reynolds, he's a god," she tells us. "And Nicky Avery—he'll be sitting with the band nerds, he's the only cute one. And look for Sandra, she's in my row, she let her mother cut her hair yesterday and now she looks like a total *boy*. She said she was thinking of blowing the whole thing off."

But of course Sandra will not do anything of the kind: she is there with all the others as I pull into the parking lot, dozens of kids milling outside the doors, boys in blue robes and girls in white, mugging for cameras and fiddling with caps and gowns and tassels, the buzz of nervous laughter spreading throughout the crowd and into the vacant hallways of the school. I see a bunch of other girls like Francie, who have polished their fingernails silver and used white spray paint on the bobby pins that hold the flimsy mortarboards in their hair. The four of us in our family stand in a circle as Elaine adjusts the collar on Francie's robe, and for a final time I open my mouth to show I have something to say, but Francie has already turned her back to me and joined the white sorority on its way into the building. Teachers stand among the students, holding clipboards and trying to check off names, and I watch for one of them to tap Francie on the shoulder and take her aside; but the sentinels are finally reduced to helpless shrugs and smiles as the graduates swell and chatter through the doors. I watch them flow away like a field of angels, and wish I had the courage to confess to them my secret.

"Let's go," Jill says with urgency, sounding a lot like her mother. She leads the way through the doors of the gym foyer, and I follow my family down the stairs to the basketball floor, where people wait on clean wax to climb up the bleachers and claim their seats. We step across other families, some we have known for years and others we are acquainted with only through events like this. They all look familiar to me, and I can tell from the approving reflections in their faces that they recognize us in the same way.

I pick up my program to fan myself in the hot closed air, but first I take a look at the list inside, and there is *Frances L. Griffith* just where it should be, under "Graduating Class" between *Gorman* and *Grimeldi*. I feel a flash of relief, then realize that the programs must have been printed before exams were graded. I fold the page back, making a crease out of my name, and wonder if there might still be time to spring down the steps and out into the hall to snatch Francie away, as if saving her from gunfire.

But now as the music starts the room is thick with bodies, packing everyone together, and we all stand to watch the robed flanks approaching. The girls file in through one door and the boys through another, and they meet halfway to form their rows and march to the folding chairs set up in military smartness beneath the scoreboard. Elaine grabs my arm and pokes herself in the cheek, by accident, with the hard corner of her program. "There she is," she says, pointing, but I have already located Francie, in a middle row, whispering with excitement to the girls on either side of her. "She's shaking," Elaine adds, and I believe she does know this for a fact, even though Francie is really too far away for us to see that clearly.

At the end of the processional it occurs to me that this may not be a disaster, after all. In fact, I may have actually done Francie a favor by not telling her what I know. When Jill graduated from this high school, the students didn't receive their diplomas until after the ceremony—they handed the principal little cards with their names on them to be read over the microphone, and they were handed empty diploma covers in return. If they do it the same way now, it means Francie won't be losing anything until afterward, when she tries to exchange her cap and gown for the official certificate, and in the meantime I will be able to intercept her and explain. It will hurt more than I can guess, but at least she'll have her part in this celebration, the farewell she thinks is final.

After I convince myself of this, I manage to take a deep breath into my gut, and I listen to the valedictory address from Michael Looby, who went to nursery school with Francie and once broke his arm, by running away from her, at a birthday party in our back yard. Michael speaks of beginnings and endings and spirit and ambition and debt, and around us the other parents are nodding and smiling and whispering to each other, and Elaine and I do the same, but for a different reason: we are remembering the broken arm, and how Michael ran away from Francie a second time when she went at him with a crayon brandished to sign the cast.

I look at Francie poking at her hair, pulling it out of her collar and smoothing it behind her ears, and I think how well the hairband could serve her now. But she might not want it; the butterflies suddenly seem childish, and might not match what she is wearing. I was never good at knowing things like that. On the bleacher seat, I shift hard and wish I'd bought her a jumbo package of Mallo Cups instead. When she was little, I could give her these to get her to stop crying.

As soon as the speakers are through and the graduates step forward, I listen to the first few names and feel my sweat begin to rise. The students are responding to the sound of their names being recited by the principal, in alphabetical order. "What happened to the little name cards?" I say frantically, and Jill's look tells me I have been louder than I planned.

"Dad, get a grip, okay?" she whispers, slouching down

in her seat. "They changed it this year. There's just one big list they read from."

They are approaching the D's, and my tongue is dry. How can I save her now? Could I try to swoop down and tuck her beneath my arm, and escape flying through the rafters to the roar of the arena?

Elaine notices that there is something wrong with me. "You're making noise," she tells me, as my breath comes out in voice. I try to stop doing this and she seems satisfied, though she still gives me an odd look from her profile.

They continue their countdown: E, F, G. I say the letters in my mind to the tune of the child's alphabet song. Francie's row rises and I watch her fingering her hair, preparing to fall into line. What will she do when the principal calls *Gorman* and then—as Francie steps forward with a self-conscious toss of her hair—the name of the girl who stands in line behind her? There will be a swift moment of shock and confusion, I am sure of that. I consider faking a heart attack or some other emergency to divert the crowd, but then I realize that this would be even more embarrassing to my daughter.

What will she do? Will she flush with shame and discovery, and stumble to the side of the gym in her high white shoes, and look for her mother to console her? Or will she—in that instant when her name is not called—realize what has happened and what she will have to do in remedy, and walk with a calm smile and clear face back to her row, and make a snide remark about algebra to her friends?

"They're coming to us, now," Elaine warns me, grabbing onto my shoulder. I lift my nose against a sour smell, until I recognize the leak of my own breath in the air around us. "Sarah Marie Gorman," the principal intones. Then, after a pause that presses my heart back into itself, the name only I am expecting, in a solemn, near-holy tone: "Theresa Grimeldi."

"Wait—*what*?" Elaine rustles beside me, and shoots up to get a better look at the floor. "What happened? Where is she? They skipped right over her name!"

"Ssh," somebody behind us says, but Elaine doesn't care. Instead she turns to look down at me. "What the hell?" she says, as if she knows I have the answer, and I have no choice but to stand up, too.

"Look," Jill says, pointing to the EXIT sign, "there she is." Elaine and I look just in time to see the white robe retreating, the folds flapping around Francie's stiffly rapid legs.

"Could you please sit down?" The voice in the back of the bleachers is more insistent, and turning I see the hostile poppy field of faces aimed up at us, no longer smiling.

"Oh, shut up," Elaine tells them under her breath. She puts her foot down on the bleacher seat, catching another woman's skirt under her sandal, and begins a slow, forward descent. The people move aside to make an annoyed narrow path as they feel her coming, and they stay leaning against each other until Jill and I follow her through, leaving behind us a low chorus of excuse me's.

In the hallway we find Francie with her back pressed flat against the wall, palms crossed in front of her thighs, staring down at the silver toenails lined up across the front of her open shoes. She doesn't look up as we come closer, although she seems aware that we are all here. "Francie— what happened?" Elaine says. "Honey, did they just forget to call you? How could they screw something like this up?"

"I don't know," Francie says, still looking down, but in her voice I hear the possibility that maybe she does know.

"Francie," I begin, but that's all I can manage. Nobody seems to be waiting for anything more; it's as if I've offered as much as they could expect of me. We all stand there not knowing what to say next, as a janitor sliding his wide brush in our direction looks over and switches lanes halfway down the hall, though that side's already clean, to avoid the obstruction we make.

"I think maybe I flunked my algebra," Francie says, finally. "Then I wouldn't have enough credits. That's what happened to Hillary Whiting."

Jill says, "But wouldn't they have told you? That you weren't on the list?"

The corridor we stand in is a long tunnel, turning dim as the sun sinks, with a round shine of light at the end, where the entrance is. I feel as if I should be gathering my family close around me, guiding them down through the dark toward safety, emerging first to make sure the night outside is friendly. But instead we all stand there without moving until Elaine says, "Do you think we should wait now to find out what the story is? Or—"

"Let's just go home," Francie says, and Elaine nods, having already guessed.

"What a bunch of idiots," my wife says, as I nose the car slowly into the street. "I still can't believe they could make such a stupid mistake." She looks out her window intently, as if a solution will be hanging on a tree branch.

"You guys," I say, turning into the driveway, letting the car stall to a stop. "Listen." I can't even make out their faces as they turn to me, indistinct in the dark.

"Listen," I say again, but by then they are already outside the car, shutting all the doors firmly on their way into the house.

Hours later I am sitting in front of the TV, nursing a beer, eating another piece of the graduation cake. Not because I am still hungry, but because there's nothing more tartly sweet to me than the taste of fudge frosting mixed with cold beer. Everyone else is asleep except for Francie, who decided, after being alone with the phone in her bedroom for an hour, to go to the parties with Hillary Whiting. She left with swollen eyes, but her face was calm, and her movement out the door was numbly graceful, like a dancer too proud to show she has been injured. Elaine tried to comfort her as she left, but Francie kept brushing her away.

"It's no biggie," she said to us. "Hillary says there's a major god who teaches math in summer school, so we're psyched. Look, I'm late already. Don't wait up for me, okay?" She left, and Elaine went to bed soon afterward, without telling me good night.

But it's my habit to be here in my chair this late, sitting in front of the TV set, drinking a beer. Something about being awake, while the world around me is unconscious and vulnerable, lets me finally relax. Tonight the late movie is about a painful disease that kills most of the people in a small town, and the tragedy is so contrived it makes me smile. It's almost over, film dissolving into fuzz at the end of the broadcast day, when there is a noise at the back door and I hear Francie coming into the house, pausing to drop her shoes at the top of the stairwell. I hear her open the cupboards and then the fridge, and when she comes to the family room door I see she is holding a can of my Bud.

"Hey," I say, then decide I will go easy. "Don't let your mother see you drinking that. She'll hold me accountable."

"Don't worry." She pops it open, expertly keeping the sound down by holding a pressed finger against the tab. "What's on?" She is looking at the blank screen, taking a hefty swig. I realize, watching, that of course this bitterness is nothing new to her: she drinks without flinching, seems even to welcome the taste.

"Nothing. I mean, it's over now." I reach for the remote, but then she is unmistakably crying, and I keep the TV on so she won't be the only sound in a silent room. "What's the matter?" I ask, stupidly, as her long hair trembles on top of her folded arms.

"Dad, I'm so sorry," she says, and her voice is that buzzy mixture of beers and sorrow. "I didn't mean to flunk. Didn't I embarrass you and Mom? Aren't you guys extremely pissed off?"

She's too far away for me to reach without moving, so I get up out of my chair and sit down again, next to where she is standing in the doorway. At the side of my eye I see her start to lean away, but then she fumbles her beer as she drops to her knees and pitches her face into my shoulder. I feel the foam spreading inside my socks, like blood from a cut I forgot to take care of. I try to tell myself that she won't find out about my betrayal until tomorrow, but at the same time I realize, hearing the TV fade, that it is tomorrow already.

I hand her my own beer, and she sucks at it noisily. "It's okay," I tell her, hearing my voice plead. "Like you said, it's no biggie. Okay?"

"Okay," she says. Or at least that's what I think I hear; the word is lost in a slurp and swallow. She wipes her mouth with her hand and offers me the beer back, and we share the rest of it like this, laughing sadly as it gets emptier, slowing down the sips, neither of us wanting to be the one to finish it.

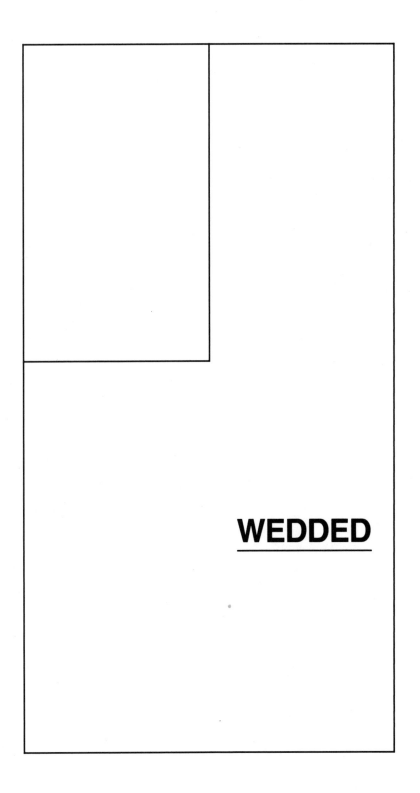

WEDDED

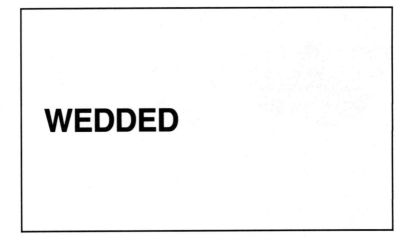

WEDDED

My fingers bled, but the prick-marks meant *I love you.*
The tucking, folding, and stitching had gotten to be a
rhythm, silent and soothing, and when the doorbell rang I
jerked a little, losing my thread. I heard a quick exchange
of laughs and chatter downstairs at the front door, and then
my sister said "Thanks again" and shut it. Neighbors had
been bringing gifts over to the house all week; the dining
room table was piled high with gold and silver packages. It
made me nervous, wanting to knock wood, to see so many
BEST WISHES winking out among the wrappings. My sister
called it sweet.

Francie was getting married the next day, and the presents were for her. She didn't usually have much to be
worried about, and she wouldn't have wanted me to know
she was worried now, but older sisters can see the signs.
When she came upstairs and into our old bedroom, she
was plucking Triscuits straight out of the box in handfuls,
which is a sign, because normally she is a dainty eater. But
now she chewed so fast her words came out in whistles.

"I figure I won't eat anything tomorrow," she said, not
even offering me the box. "If I do, I know I'll throw up
halfway down the aisle. Can you imagine?" But I couldn't.
Not Francie: she was born with the gift of charm, and it
would take more than a mere wedding to spoil her spell.

"Hey, France." Our mother called up from the bottom of
the stairs. "The groom's here. He looks a little tense. I think

maybe he wants to call it off." Then we heard our mother's nervous laughter greeting Greg, who would vow himself into the family tomorrow. At the rehearsal dinner, he and Francie had excused themselves from the table before dessert, and I found them fifteen minutes later, kissing behind the rubber plant in the restaurant foyer.

"We're going out with everybody. Wanna come?" Francie peered into the mirror, bared her small teeth and picked cracker crumbs from between them. "Everybody" meant the friends of hers and Greg's who had come to serve as bridesmaids and ushers—girls who still had pimples to conceal, boys who still drank beer as if it were something to get away with.

"No, thanks," I said. "Finger probably will, though." My boyfriend had come home with me for the wedding, and he had trouble finding things we would allow him to do.

"Okay. Listen, Jill, promise me something? If you see Dad getting hammered tomorrow, make him stop. Take him away, stitch his lips together, I don't care what. Just don't let him make a scene. Okay?" Now she was putting on lip gloss, spreading shininess across pink.

"Why don't you ever believe what people tell you? Mom says she hasn't seen him drunk in a long time. He asks for juice now, when he comes over."

"Yeah, right. *Juice*," Francie grumbled, clearly doubtful. She tapped my shoulder with the Triscuit box, set it on the table and left the room. I considered taking a break to eat some crackers, but decided I didn't want to get crumbs in my way. The something borrowed would be my long slip, and I was taking it in to fit my sister, tapering the waistline, smoothing out the lace.

Later, I went downstairs to the living room, where my mother was sitting around drinking gin-and-tonics with Genevieve, who had lived in the house next to ours until six months ago. Genevieve was a photographer, and she had promised to take pictures of the wedding party and candids at the reception. Her daughter, Sam, who was ten and

who would be a junior bridesmaid, was standing in bore-
dom by the piano, plinking notes without a tune.

"Jilly, there you are," Genevieve said, as I sat down on
the piano bench next to the box of unused wedding invita-
tions Francie had ordered the wrong way the first time,
asking for *Mr. and Mrs. Arthur Griffith request*, instead of
the separated version using *Arthur and Elaine*. "Let the
gossip begin. We were just talking about the Relihans."
They were our neighbors at the end of the street, a Catholic
family of two parents and six children who all had first
names beginning with *M*. Mr. Relihan was also the father of
the baby belonging to Cheryl Lucas, who lived around the
corner, and the only people who didn't seem aware of this
were the rest of the Relihans.

"Do you think Mary Relihan can possibly be that oblivi-
ous?" Genevieve was asking. "I heard she made booties
for that baby. And she offered to *sit* with him if Cheryl's
ever in a pinch." I noticed that Genevieve's voice had taken
on a light Southern broadness since she moved down to
Georgia, over the winter, after her own divorce. The demure
new accent didn't quite go with her clothes, which were the
same old Genevieve, a crazy caftan, flowing paisley scarf,
and huge silver hoop earrings that could have served
equally well as Christmas tree ornaments.

She went on. "How long do you think it'll be before she
catches on?" She was swirling her drink with a ringed
finger. "His car is parked in front of Cheryl's every other
night. You'd think he could *walk* a block, for the sake of
discretion. But no, he practically ties a red ribbon around
his—uh, member."

"Member of what?" Sam asked.

"It's a grown-up thing, honey," Genevieve told her.

I waited for my mother to be embarrassed, but instead
she leaned closer to Genevieve on the couch and said, "A
blue ribbon is more like it," and they giggled, and though
part of me felt like smiling too, I could see Sam shifting next
to me in disgust.

"Maybe she loves him," she suggested, suspending for

a moment her fingers above the keyboard. "His wife. Did you ever think of that?"

"Samantha," Genevieve said, in a warning tone.

"Oh, forget it," Sam said, leaving the piano with a discordant punch. "You never let me say anything." She went into the guest bedroom, and we heard the door close with a loud click just short of a slam.

"Jesus." Genevieve leaned back toward my mother and confided, "You were so smart to wait until your kids were older and on their own. I think she'll be making me pay for this divorce until she can grow up and get one for herself."

"You really have gotten cynical, Gen," my mother said. "Maybe she'll get married and wind up happily ever after."

"Yeah, and maybe I'll become Pope." Genevieve spat a piece of ice back into her glass. "At least in your case it wasn't another woman. Art still worships the pot you pee in, Elaine."

"Don't be gross. Besides, you haven't even seen him in six months."

"Well, before we moved, I could tell. When he'd come over to see the kids, or fix the car, I could see it in the way he watched you. Sometimes when you went back into the house, he'd just look at the door for a whole minute before he went back to what he was doing. Daydreaming, like. Staring at nothing, except where you'd been."

"Oh, get out of here."

"It's true." Genevieve was grinning. "So how about it? Would you ever take him back?"

My mother looked down into her drink. Now she was embarrassed.

I told her, "Anything you say can and will be used against you in a court of law."

"Honestly, you two." My mother began tapping her glass against the sofa. "Actually, all he talks about is getting back together. But I've hoped too many times to ever trust him again. He may have stopped drinking for a while, but it'll get him sooner or later. It always does." She finished with a gulp. "I wish I didn't believe that, but I do."

" 'Oh, ye of little faith,' " Genevieve pronounced, and my mother said, "Damn straight."

"Does anybody want anything?" Generally I like women talk, but this was making me feel privy to secrets I didn't deserve to hear. I got up and started toward the kitchen. "Pepsi, Sam?" I called, in the direction of the guest room.

The door opened and Sam came out slowly. She moved into the living room and shook her head at me. She had been drawing with colored pens in the fleshy web of her hand, between her thumb and first finger, and she held it up to show us a face with flowers for eyes and a mouth shaped like a heart. She looked over at her mother, and then out the window into the late warm darkness of summer, where crickets shrieked across the strip of grass that used to be her playground.

"So who's living in our house now?" she asked us casually, making her fingers move as if the heart were talking. "Who's sleeping in my room?"

Finger got back from the bar caravan before the rest of them. He came in to kiss me good night before he would go downstairs to the family room, where he had pitched a sleeping bag on the floor. "Are you stinking?" I asked him, watching his shadow come toward me in the dark. It was late. My mother had gone to bed hours ago, and I stayed up only a little longer, reminiscing with Sam and Genevieve.

" 'Oh, ye of little faith,' " he said, echoing Genevieve, and I felt the twinge caused by a chance meeting of moments that means something, though we never figure out what it is. "I only stayed for a couple of toasts. But your sister's committing major brain cell abuse." He put the full weight of his body on the single bed beside me, and we rolled toward each other in the middle, laughing but trying not to make noise. "Too bad I'm not just a little crocked," he went on, grabbing my breast under my nightshirt, "or I'd stay here with you, and not care about who hears us."

"Oh," I said, touching him back. "I know. I'm sorry." He pulled me closer and I breathed in frustration against his cheek. "We can't, though. Listen. My mother will wake up." I put a palm up to his lips and he laughed again, tickling my skin.

"How do you know?" he asked.

"Because we used to hear *them*."

"When?"

"After he moved out. Before, never. Maybe they weren't doing it." I paused, trying to recall what tenderness between my parents had looked like. "But after he left, and they started—what would you call it, dating? it sounds silly—he'd stay over after he brought her home. I guess they were both lonely. Anyway, they'd be loud. Like they were hurting each other."

"Did they know you could hear?" He had lifted his arm around the top of my head, and he began stroking my hair.

"No. He always left before we got up. I guess they wanted to keep us innocent." I spread strands of my hair out across his chest, because he liked this, and then I laughed. "Thank God it didn't work."

"You think they'll ever get back together? Do you want them to?" Finger's parents had a marriage that wouldn't quit, and he sometimes asked me questions about my family as if it were a new subject for him to study, of anthropological intrigue.

"I don't know. I don't know," I said to both questions, afraid to answer further. He began kissing me again, and I let him go deeper, burrowing his face against my neck.

"And what about us?" he whispered, already knowing that I wouldn't let him leave.

In the morning, everybody was up early and convened around boxed coffee cake at the kitchen table. The house was taut with the clatter of nerves and hands fumbling. Genevieve, flamboyant in a long gypsy dress and red ankle boots, kept popping out of her chair during breakfast to take pictures of us all doing nervous things; Francie stirring her coffee with a barrette, our mother sticking the top of the juice can in the toaster. Genevieve told Sam to wash off the face she'd drawn the night before on her fingers, but Sam refused. "It's for the wedding," she said. "It's part of my disguise."

"You mean outfit," Genevieve said. "Well, if you get ink poisoning, don't blame me."

Francie spent the hour following breakfast at the vanity table, doing her hair, and as I watched her I saw that she was still my vain little sister in the familiar ways. When she knelt before the mirror, trying to find the right angle to fit her contact lenses, her movements so resembled an act of genuflection that I looked away to let her worship in private. "Scared?" I asked when she was finished, and she turned to smile, her eyes shining with wetness that could have been bottled saline or real tears.

"To death," she said. "What if something goes wrong?"

"It won't," I said, knowing she meant the marriage itself, and not the wedding. "*Somebody* has to live happily ever after."

At the church there was a single car, our father's, parked next to the building when we arrived in the station wagon, all of us packed like glass within the cushion of wedding dresses and Genevieve's camera gear. Our mother drove in and parked next to our father's car, where he was sitting in the driver's seat with his head back and his eyes closed, listening to a radio talk show about child arsonists. When he saw us he turned off the radio, and got out in a hurry. He was sweating under his armpits and carried his tux jacket over his shoulder.

"Didn't want to go in alone," he told us, kissing Francie first, and then our mother and me. "Thought I might get the urge to pray or something, and who knows where that could lead." We laughed, because this was purely our father talking, with no evidence of alcohol in his manner or his breath. "Genevieve! How the hell are you?" He went behind our mother to give our old neighbor a hug, and she patted the back of his sweat-stained shirt, her thick rings thumping with affection on the fabric.

"Hi, Art," she said. "It's good to see you. You're taking care, I see."

"You noticed?" He did look trim; he hadn't had a drink in months, he'd been careful to tell us all. The old paunch around his waist had thinned into a firm midriff. He and Genevieve locked arms and followed the others toward the church, and I caught their murmured exchange behind me as I walked beside Finger. "Is this a bitch, or what?" my father said.

"What, weddings? Oh, you mean breaking up. A definite bitch," Genevieve agreed, laughing.

"A definite goddam bitch," Sam murmured, tapping her patent leather toes across the pavement.

"Cool it, Sam," Genevieve told her.

"Sam? *Sam*? This grown-up girl is the infamous Silly Sam?" Our father halted as if stunned, and bent over to peer closely at Sam's face, which was wrinkled with suspicions.

"You know it's me," she said.

"Well, it's true, I had a hunch. But you've grown up since the last time I saw you. Is that a *dress* you're wearing?" I heard that his voice had regained its familiar charm.

"No, it's a garbage can," Sam said.

"Samantha, I'm warning you."

"I see she inherited your tongue, too," my father said to Genevieve. "Look out, world."

Inside the church, Genevieve bent down to attach a flash to her camera. Later the picture would show us all standing stiffly together, shoulders rubbing, brows furrowed above smiles. Then the bridesmaids arrived together from the hotel, escorted by the ushers, and the dressing rooms of the church filled with the sounds of hysterical chatter and the scent of powder, cigarettes, and perfume. Soon the front doors of the church were opened to the bright noon, and the guests began filing into the pews. Peeking through the sanctuary doors, I recognized the faces of neighbors, Francie's classmates, people from my mother's office, and my parents' married friends. The Relihans took up a whole row, from Martin to Madeleine, and Mrs. Relihan was whispering something to her husband, and he was smiling at whatever it was. Everyone looked fancy and unnaturally enthused. I leaned against the wall of the pastor's study, and overheard the voices of my parents inside.

"Thanks," my mother was saying.

"Where'd you get it?"

"Macy's." So they were talking about my mother's dress. "Jill helped me pick it out."

"She's gotten some good taste. She looks great lately, by the way. She's lost weight, hasn't she? And her skin looks better."

"Why don't you tell her? She'd love to hear that."

"Think so?" I heard my father flick his lighter and suck hugely, the way he always started cigarettes. "I didn't think it would matter, coming from me." My mother let this pass, and I was grateful. "Her boyfriend seems like a good guy," my father went on. "But what kind of a name is Finger, for God's sake?"

"I didn't want to ask," my mother said, and I believed I could hear her mouth work its way into a grin. "You've met him before, though. He came home with her for New Year's Eve."

"Oh, right." But I knew he didn't remember that blurry night. "So are they going to get hitched too, or what?"

"I don't know. She hasn't said one way or the other."

"I suppose if they've got a good thing going, why ruin it?"

I smiled, thinking of Finger and the night before. "We did a good job, I guess, didn't we?" my father said then.

"What, the girls?"

"Yeah. I mean, they turned out okay. A few rough times, but at least neither of them ever had a baby or got arrested or anything." There was a pause, more smoking. "It was mainly because of you, though. How many dinners did I miss? Jesus, to think of everything I kissed away in that goddam bar."

"Let's not talk about it today." Against my father's agitation, my mother's voice was calm.

"Okay." My father lit a new cigarette and asked, "Did anybody remember to bring rice?"

"Oh, my God. I bet they forgot. Maybe they'll have to throw confetti, like at ours."

"Remember that? Will and Rita ripped up their programs and dropped them from the ledge. You kept shrugging your head around to get rid of it. I thought I'd married a spaz."

"Well, it was sticking to my veil." I heard my mother laugh and then catch her breath. "Maybe that's what jinxed us, you think?"

"No. Everything we said that day, I meant. I still mean."

"I meant it too then. *Then*," she told him.

I stopped listening, but not in time to keep the pinch out of my heart. Finger found me and drew me away. We all swished, whispering, to the sanctuary foyer, as the organist began the cues she had taught us the night before. At the altar, my father deposited Francie at Greg's side, and took a few steps backward to join my mother, who stood alone in the front pew. The ceremony followed dim as a dream, and I watched the colored glass of the windows waver in front of my eyes. During a silent point in the service, I heard the sounds of imploded giggling, and expected to see one of the bridesmaids losing control; but looking around I saw that it was my mother making the sounds, with her face shaking behind her handkerchief. My father's cheeks were red, and for a moment I was afraid he'd start laughing too, but in the next instant he saved us. Just by reaching down to touch our mother's hand, he made her cry instead.

The reception was being held back at our house, in the garden my father gave my mother two years ago, a farewell gesture, or maybe one last try, the summer he moved out. Near the hyacinth bed, behind a table stacked high with napkins that said "Frances and Gregory" around the borders, Finger was being an informal bartender, and guests milled around us, eating stuffed mushrooms and cherry tomatoes, laughing, clinking glasses. My mother ordered a gin-and-tonic and Finger poured it for her, heavy on the gin. "You deserve this," he told her, handing it over.

My father appeared at my mother's elbow and shoved it gently. "What kind of example is this for the children?" he said with a smile, imitating a line of hers from long ago. He had been following her around, back down the aisle and now home from the church, like a schoolboy enamored of a new teacher. "I'll have a glass of juice if you've got it, Finger," he said. "You kids have seen enough corruption for one day." When he took the glass, he hesitated a moment, then threw his head back and gulped mightily, sweat snaking down his neck. I watched the motion with a shiver. This was how he used to drink his beer, first poised at the edge of decorum, then diving reckless into the fog.

"That's good," my mother said, also watching. "I'm glad for you, you know, Art." She seemed to be edging away from him, but at the same time her eyes lingered on his face, which was indisputably handsome and clear again, unswelled, and free of inner shadows.

"Hey, you guys, give me a smile." Genevieve had crept up with her camera, and was sighting my parents together through the viewfinder. I saw that my mother smiled with tight lips each time the two of them were clicked into focus. "Don't worry, just a throwaway to finish off the roll. Nobody will see it and get the wrong idea," Genevieve said, wandering off toward Sam and the Relihan children, who were playing croquet in the yard.

"Art, hell of a party," somebody said, passing by and jostling my father's arm. It was Dick Keveney, who used to be my parents' lawyer before they got separate ones.

"Thanks, Dick. Hey, you know how daughters are, buddy. This one may break me," my father said, tapping Francie's arm as she twirled by with Greg. "What's the matter now?" he said then, as my mother pulled away.

"Oh, come on. It's just so typical, you taking the credit. I've been saving up for a year now to pay for all of this." I looked down as my mother's eyes narrowed, and felt my breath break on the rise. Across the bar, I could see Finger watching us, sympathetic and curious.

"I offered to help out."

"I didn't want you to. But I guess I might as well have, with everybody congratulating *you*."

"I thought you were the one who didn't want to fight today."

"Fine."

"So dance with me?" My father put his glass down and extended a hand to my mother, who stammered momentarily, flushing, before taking his hand and letting him swing her away, her feet grazing the grass. The band, a quartet of graduate students called The Academia Nuts, was playing "Is You Is or Is You Ain't My Baby?" My parents moved easily to a private cadence, my father's lips grazing my mother's hair as he whispered the lyrics through the song. But in the middle my mother stopped abruptly and turned away, and strode awkwardly in her long dress back to the bar. She picked up her drink and finished it quickly.

"What's the matter?" Finger asked her. "It was looking good from here."

"He just won't give up. We can't even have a simple dance together without him proposing all over the place." The p's were making her spit.

"He proposed?" Finger, pouring another gin, looked up, surprised and hopeful for me.

"Oh, he's always doing that. I thought you knew, Jill? He just won't take no for an answer. I'm going in to change." She took the drink he'd mixed her, and went into the house.

"God," Finger said. "I didn't know there was a chance they might—"

"There isn't," I told him, and also myself. "He just wants to believe there is."

I was fixing Finger's tie, which didn't need fixing, when Genevieve approached, trailing a cranky Sam. "Somebody whacked her ball into a pile of dog shit, right when she was about to win," Genevieve explained. "I told her, get used to it. That's life."

"Guess what," I said. "Dad just proposed to Mom again. Whoops—everybody shut up—he's coming over here."

"Hi, Gen. Hi, sweetie pie," my father said, leaning down to look Sam in the eyes. "What's the matter? Why such a long pout on that pretty face?"

"Because your lawn is full of dog shit," she replied.

"Sam, goddammit," Genevieve said.

"Mommy, you swore." Sam smirked back and reached for a ginger ale. The face painted in pen between her fingers was fading in the heat, the colors running together to make a pretty bruise. Behind us, the band began to play a fast version of "What I Like About You."

"Gen, want to try this one?" my father asked her. "I seem to have lost my partner for the moment. Please? For old times' sake?" They moved out onto the dance floor, where Francie and Greg and their friends were already stepping high, slapping their palms together, bobbing their heads. My father and Genevieve got into it, he twisting his shiny heels up, she kicking her short red boots behind her. They flicked off so much energy that gradually the younger dancers began to spread out around them, making them the center of the floor, the way Francie and Greg had commanded all eyes during the first slow dance. When it was over everybody clapped, and my father followed Genevieve over to the bar again, where my mother, dressed in a cooler skirt and blouse, was sipping another drink.

"Here's to Fred and Ginger," she said, lifting her glass to them. "I guess I'm out of it. You couldn't get me to move like that if you set my underwear on fire."

"It's not really that big a deal, Elaine," Genevieve said, pouring herself a beer. "You just do whatever feels right."

"Look, Mom, your pits are sweating," Sam pointed out.

"Your mom was great!" My father bent over again to Sam, and my mother looked at me watching them together, the girl without a father, and the man who tried to make her smile. "I bet someday she'll teach you how to dance like that, too. I bet you'll have so many boys wanting to dance with you it'll make you spin."

"Art," my mother said, "could you come here a minute?" She had moved over near the azaleas at the edge of the yard. At first they mumbled, but then my mother's voice began scaling shrill and trembly. Finger raised his eyes in a question at me, but I couldn't answer. "Do you have to spend so much time fawning over someone else's daughter, when you have two of your own conveniently within speaking range? One of whom, by the way, has just gotten married? You never paid either of them this much attention when they were Samantha's age."

"Elaine, maybe you've had enough."

"Oh, okay, now *I'm* the one who drinks. That's good. Oh, I like that."

"Elaine—" his voice was low but urgent—"can't you see how I've been changing? I keep trying to prove it to you. I know I screwed up before. For twenty years! I wanted to start over. I wanted—another chance." Across the yard, I found myself straining to catch every word, along with the other people who had stalled their conversations and were pretending not to listen.

"Well, you'll have to get it from somebody else, then." I had no trouble hearing my mother. "You've always been a great date, Art, but you're a lousy husband."

My father's face flinched at this, but his body remained steady. "Come on, put that drink down, okay? You want to go for a walk?"

"With you?"

"Just around the corner. Get some fresh air."

"I will not."

"Why?"

"I just won't!" This came out on the order of a shriek, and some of the guests began to look over now to where my parents were standing. I saw Mary Relihan whisper behind her hand. I felt in one instant compelled to break them up, and in the next helpless to think of how I might do so. I looked at Finger and he came over to put his hand on mine, but he had no solution either.

"I will not let you charm me into this. It's Mr. Nice Guy

this, Mr. Nice Guy that in public. But you haven't changed, you couldn't. As soon as we got alone you'd go back to the way you always were, staying out till dawn and stumbling home all drunk and sorry in the morning."

Her voice began to quaver even more. "Do you remember where you were the night Francie was born? I had to leave Jill at your mother's and have her track you down. Do you think you could have stayed sober, just for one night? She even came on her due date, to make it easier for you. But no—that was too much to ask." She drew up her shoulders in a mix of indignation and shame, and walked away from him. Too late, the band consulted hurriedly and struck up "A Couple of Swells." Francie came over tottering on her high white heels."

"What the hell was that little show for?" she demanded. "Are they trying to ruin my life?"

My mother stalked inside the house, and Genevieve followed her. Dick Keveney made a joke. As the guests started up a nervous babble, my father came over to me and said, "I've had about all I can handle. Sorry, sweetheart. I'll be back later."

"Where are you going?" I could hear the panic leaking through my voice.

"Nowhere. Don't worry. Just out for a drive, that's all." He walked around to the front of the house, and I saw that his shirt had begun to come untucked from his cummerbund. A few minutes later his car chugged out of the driveway and down the street, the sounds of talk show static trailing out the window.

I went into the house and found my mother lying on the sofa. Genevieve was putting a cloth across her forehead. "I feel better now," my mother said. "I threw up."

"Good."

"Where did your father go?"

"I don't know. Just for a drive, he said."

"If he comes back here drunk, I don't know what I'll do."

"He won't. Anyway, people are supposed to drink at weddings. Look at—well, let's face it, *you*."

"No, thank you," my mother said. "What do you bet he'll be completed wasted by the time he comes back? If he comes back at all?"

"He'll be back, Elaine," Genevieve said.

"You know he can't handle it when we fight. I've had it, being responsible for his benders." She stretched out further on the sofa. "Maybe somebody should keep an eye out for when he gets here. Poor Francie. I'm too sick to feel guilty now, but this is going to kill me in the morning."

I went back outside, but I didn't feel like being there, either. I found Finger and took him away from the bar, and we danced to a slow tune. "My father wants to know if we're getting married," I told him.

"What did you say?"

"It wasn't me he asked, it was my mother. I guess I would have said the answer is maybe." We had both thought about it and not talked about it since the day we met, two years ago in August, waiting on a platform for a train that never came. He was ugly, which made me trust him and not care about how I looked, and then I loved him, and he wasn't ugly anymore.

He propelled me around in a circle. "I love you," he told me, and I remembered that things could be right, and safe, and I closed my eyes against his collar, letting him hold me.

After a while my mother came out again, asking for a ginger ale. People sat down at their places at the long table, and everybody ate, and toasted the bride and groom with champagne. After the meal, Greg and Francie disappeared, and I found them around the side of the house, kissing behind the woodpile. My lace slip was dragging under Francie's skirt in the dirt. "I don't mean to interrupt," I said, after clearing my throat.

"Yes, you do," Francie told me. "What's the matter? Are they selling tickets to the next round?"

"I think you should cut the cake. People are waiting."

"Oh, yeah. Okay." Francie reached down and pulled Greg up by his lapel, and they both fell against the side of the house, laughing. "Did you notice that the candy bride does look a lot like me?"

She was flopping pieces of the cake onto outstretched plates when our father's car limped back onto the street and into the driveway. He got out and leaned against the house, watching us all from a distance. My mother and I saw him at the same time, and my mother dropped her napkin and started to go to him, her movements speaking protest. But he put his hand up as if to ward her off, and came over to the head table. When Francie saw him, she stopped slicing little ragged lines of entry across the cake.

"Hi, Daddy," she said, and giggled. Greg took the knife from her and reached over to shake our father's hand.

"Didn't really get a chance to say much to you earlier, Mr.—Art," he said. "At the church, I mean."

"True enough, Mr. Greg. Well, welcome to our family. Such as it is." My father shook Greg's hand, and then turned to my mother. "Like father, like daughter, I always say," he told her, smiling at Francie, who was trying to spread her husband's face with a knifeful of vanilla. But my father himself had not, in his absence, been drinking; I could tell by his straight smile and the peculiar veinless clarity of his eyes.

"Have a piece of cake, Art," my mother said, unsurely.

"I want one of the roses," Sam said, holding up her plate.

"Isn't she adorable?" My father caught my mother's eye and added, "Almost as cute as ours, Lainie." He turned to me. "By the way, Jill honey, have I told you how pretty you've gotten?" he said, and I smiled, not wanting to let him know about the stab his effort gave me. My father picked an entire sugar rose off the top of the cake and plopped it onto Sam's plate. "Sweets to the sweet," he said.

"Art—"

"Certainly, I am going to have a piece. But first, a small wish for the happy couple." He drew an orange box of Uncle Ben's converted long grain rice out of his suit pocket, and punched open the little spout on the side.

"Hey, yeah, rice! We forgot." Sam put her cake down,

made her palms into cups and held them upward. "Can I throw some?"

"In a minute," he told her. "As father of the bride, I'm pulling rank." He poured a fistful into his hand. "Here's to Francie and Greg—may their marriage last forever!" He flicked the rice up into the air, and it showered down on the table. Some of the guests laughed, and there was the sound of relieved applause from a far corner.

Genevieve moved forward to take a picture of the tribute. "Forever and ever!" he added, taking more rice, tossing it up. As his arm went high the shutter closed, and later the picture would show the rice suspended like a flat blurred galaxy as it came back down.

"Enough, now, Art," my mother told him. I heard in her voice the realization that he was sober, and her face went blankly dismal with the surprise.

"Here we go, Genevieve," my father said, drawing her over and making her pull the camera away from her face. He hugged her close with one arm, his hand open, and this time he dumped the entire contents of the box into his big palm until it overflowed. Genevieve snorted and snickered into his sleeve. "Let's do it together, now. Ready? One, two, three."

With a heavy motion of his arm, he swung his hand up and let the rice rain down like ice crystals. Genevieve laughed, until she saw my mother's face and remembered she wasn't supposed to. I felt Finger's arms closing gently around my neck and reached up to keep them there. The rice fell on the wedding cake and floated in the hot pooled wax of candles. A clump of white specks stuck in my mother's hair, and in the shadow all our faces flung across the table, I saw she wasn't even trying to shake it loose.

**ABSENT
WITHOUT
LEAVE**

ABSENT WITHOUT LEAVE

When I got to town, I tried to guess which of the three usual places I might find my father. He could have been at his apartment, flopped on the thready sofa in front of the TV, his feet with their thick yellow toenails sticking out bare beneath the comforter, a pile of Saltine-and-peanut-butter sandwiches on the milk crate table beside him; or in a back-row seat at the Alcoholics Anonymous meeting in the basement of the Reformed Church; or balanced on his lucky bar stool at the Veterans of Foreign Wars post next to the library. I figured he wouldn't be home, because he often said there was nothing more pathetic than an old boob laughing to himself in an empty living room at reruns of Gomer Pyle.

That left the AA meeting or the bar. I wondered what kind of mood he would be in, and where it would take him. The sky was gray, chilly, carrying snow in the breeze—not a day for resolutions. I drove to the VFW and found his old green Impala parked on a rough slant in the lot, and eased my own car into the space next to it. My father is not a veteran of any war, but that never seemed to matter here at the post. He has always been welcome wherever men seek brothers. On the Impala's front seat I saw a library book called *Shop for Success in the Job Market*, next to a copy of the day's newspaper folded back to the want-ad pages.

Inside the building it was dark, and I paused by the door to let my eyes adjust to the greenish sheen of the bar. I felt a chill run up my coat sleeves and into my throat, which was sore from singing with the radio for the three hours of my drive. There were five men sitting at the bar, and the middle one was my father. I hugged my arms close to myself, went over to his elbow, and said, "Dad." My father, and also the man sitting next to him, looked up with surprised heavy eyelids threaded in purple veins.

"Babe, how come you're so early?" my father said, his big hand remaining curved around the glass of flattening beer in front of him. I didn't answer and so he took the hand away, reached over to touch my arm, and leaned heavily across the stool to kiss my lips. On a ledge in the high corner, over the top shelf, men were playing basketball on television. Their jerky sprints and passes startled me in the slow-motion smoke haze of the room around us.

"Set up my daughter here, will you, Earl?" my father said to the bartender. "Hey, guys, this is my daughter, Francie. Rhyming with fancy. She lives up to the billing, wouldn't you say?" The other men nodded and smiled, and one lifted a beer toward me. I felt myself blushing in the dark. "Hon?" my father reminded me, pointing at the bartender, who stood waiting.

"A white wine, please," I told him. Until the last moment, I always thought there was the possibility that I might order a Coke instead, but I had yet to hear this surprise come out of my own mouth. I took the cold wine glass and at the first sip felt the slow warm chill spreading dependably through my blood. I shivered once, delicately, and then lifted my posture on the stool so that I was sitting above the rest of them, one straight, proud neck raised among the row of hunched dark faces gazing into their beers.

"Francie lives in Boston," my father announced. "On the so-called Freedom Trail. She's married to a lawyer—he works on Easy Street. Ha, get it?" He slapped the bar with four fingertips.

"Dad, please," I said, putting a hand on his shoulder to shush him. But nobody was paying attention anymore, because the game had come back on. The mention of

Greg and of where I had come from made me shiver again, and I felt sickness in my throat. I watched the players move up and down the floor between baskets, and at the commercial, when I looked down, I saw that my glass was empty. Before I could even signal Earl he was tilting the wine bottle in front of me, and his smile scared me, because it seemed to say he knew more about me than I intended to give away.

"Hey, I was in Boston once." I looked down at the sunglassed, white-haired man speaking from the end of the bar. It was my father's friend Ted, who began driving a bread truck after he lost his job selling cars. Once on his way home from the bar, when he was between jobs, Ted stopped at my father's apartment because he saw a light in the window, and asked my father what he was doing up so early. "It's only seven o'clock," Ted had said.

"Ted," my father told him, "it's seven o'clock *at night*."

This was a story my father liked because he thought it was funny, and it was, but I was afraid to remember it too often.

"I was at the marathon one year," Ted told the bar now, gesturing with his glass. "The year I went AWOL, after my old man died. I was driving from Maine back down to Virginia so they could catch me, and I thought I'd stop off along the way and see a few sights. The city was full of people, and I ended up by the finish line to help bring the runners home.

"It was hot out and I was sweating. We were packed like sardines. Some girl in red shorts and a bathing suit top came up to give me a kiss, and she handed me a grape Nehi. 'Thanks,' I said. 'Oh, *you're* not Jerry,' she told me, getting a better look, and I said, 'This is true.' Then I started to get nervous, wondering things like, did the U.S. military intelligence put her up to this? So I gave her back the Nehi. She looked like I'd insulted her or something. I guess she was only looking for her boyfriend, but how was I to know?" He let a fistful of peanuts drop backward into his mouth.

Another man at the bar said, "I saw that race on the tube

last year," and he slid his glass forward so Earl could hit him again. "There was this triage-type tent at the end of it, cots and blood bags wherever you cared to look. Half the people packed in ice and the rest wrapped up in tin foil like a White Castle cheeseburger. Guts, excuse me, all over the street. Now tell me, why would anyone want to put themselves through that?"

"I guess it makes them feel good," I answered, meaning it, but the men all seemed to think I was being funny. They chortled and ordered refills. My father looked proud.

"So I wasn't expecting you so soon, babe," he told me, pressing fresh foam up to his lips. Watching him sideways, I could see the flesh under his eyes swell and darken as each gulp of the beer went down.

I looked around at the shadows hanging in the room's corners, at the faces aimed rapt as lovers toward the flickery screen. "I think we should get going, Dad," I said. "It's almost time." High above us on the TV, somebody scored three points, hitting a swisher from way outside. The barroom cheered.

"You know what the beauty of this story is?" my father asked me abruptly. I didn't know what he was talking about—Ted and the marathon? a joke they had all told each other before I arrived? or something only he could hear?— so I shook my head and waited. My father leaned toward me and breathed hot beer vapors into my ear. "The beauty of this story," he whispered, "is that it *never even occurred*." I nodded, as if he had made things clear. "You see?" he insisted.

"Okay," I said, sliding off the bar stool to my feet, my boot heels hitting bare wood. "Let's go." He looked at me blankly, then suddenly recovered what I meant, as if it were a ball tapped back to the court at the last second, from its way into the stands. He raised a hand in the air and said, "Guys? See you on the rebound. I'm going to go sell my family's house."

"I thought you were all divorced now," Ted murmured, over a gentle belch.

"Ted, that's precisely the point." My father squeezed out a laugh, put a couple of dollars down and followed me out to the frozen air. Across the street was the Handi-Mart my sister and I used to shoplift Sky Bars from, and next to it the store where my mother bought me the wrong kind of gymsuit when I was in the eighth grade.

"You hear anything from Mom?" my father asked, though I had given no clues as to who I was thinking about.

"Of course," I said. "She's fine."

"Of course," he repeated. After a pause he said, "How about Jill?"

"She's fine." I felt the banality of my answer tickle my lips as it came out, and to defend myself I added, "What else can I say?"

"Not much, I guess. I tried to call her to see if she wanted us to save anything, but I got that guy Finger on the line. I don't know if he gave her my message."

"He's not just 'that guy' anymore, Dad. He's part of the family."

"What family?" He said it with a smile, but I ignored him. My windshield wipers made a screech every time they crossed the glass, giving me a headache between the eyes, but my father didn't seem to notice the noise. We drove across town and had to keep stopping for lights. Everything—the buildings, the sky, the sidewalk—looked gray and smudgy through the snow.

We passed the park, where my father had coached our Midget Miss softball team in the Tomboy League. "Just wait till a pitch feels right and then swing your heart out," he used to tell Jill and me and the other girls, but he quit when it wasn't working. We passed Hairway to Heaven, where my mother took me to have the green removed from a perm I gave myself once for the first day of school. *You'll look back and laugh at this someday*, my mother told me on the way home, and I hated her for it, though it turned out to be true.

"Remember that?" my father said, rapping the window now with the back of his hand toward the Hairway's sign, which showed a faceless head wreathed in spiral ringlets.

"You looked like the daughter from outer space." He had begun laughing again over his wheeze. I stepped a little harder on the gas pedal, and the car clattered over a hole.

"Careful," my father said.

"I *am* careful. It's just this goddam snow." I wished he would scold me for swearing, but I knew he wouldn't. We were coming up to our old road. It looked like a single private driveway, with fence arms pointing the way in; but there were four houses settled in the row, leading to a circle of gray rock and garden in front of our own place, which was the last. My mother was always fond of saying we lived on the prettiest dead end in the state. But now the grass was glazed and battered by fresh sleet, which fell with tiny taps against the windshield, making it hard to see. I said so to my father.

"You don't have to see," he told me. "Just go by feel. You could drive this road blind. God knows I've done it. That's a *joke*," he said, as I lowered my head so he wouldn't see me smile. "Honey, lighten up."

I parked in front of the garage. As I got out, wind whipped snow into my face, and I felt it melt like wet breath on the back of my neck. "Maybe we should have cancelled!" I shouted to my father, but he pointed across the road at a red Toyota with FUSCO REALTY painted into the doors.

"Too late!" he shouted back, reaching his coat high in the air, meaning he wanted to tuck me inside. I hesitated, then stooped and let him wrap it around me. We lumbered toward the house, awkward against the wind, and I could barely breathe for its power and the force of my father's breath. Through his lapel flaps I glimpsed the tire swing hanging by its frayed rope from the front yard's maple, and the post at the end of the stone walk, which used to hold a pine plaque saying that this was our house, but was now just a piece of wood stuck in the cold ground, waiting for a new name. I wondered suddenly, passionately, what had happened to the sign, the letters spelling GRIFFITH engraved in proud curved script, but I was afraid to ask. Instead I closed my eyes so I wouldn't see anything else, and let my father guide me to the door.

"I hope we get a decent one this time," he whispered into the coat. "Real estate agents tend to be losers."

Raymond Dutille was waiting for us on the front stoop, standing under a snappy black umbrella, his feet pressed tight together and a briefcase clutched to his chest. "Francie Griffith," he said as we approached the house, and he gave a smile I recognized from high school. "When I saw the appointment book, I thought it might be you." He was wearing eyeglasses that cost a lot of money, the kind on male models in fashion magazines. His shirt was pressed stiff at the collar and his coat hung straight in the hem. But underneath it all, I could tell, he was still Raymond Dutille.

"Me too," I said, though in fact I had no idea who it was we were supposed to meet, in the way of a realtor. "This is my father, Art Griffith. Dad, Raymond Dutille. We dissected a fetal pig together in ninth grade."

"Well, I hope you had better luck than my Francie, Ray," my father said, shaking hands too long, which was his habit. "If I remember right, you're a little squeamish, hon. You couldn't look at leftover spaghetti. But who am I to judge? You get that from me."

"Are we going to stand out here and chat in the hail all day, or do you think we could go inside?" My bangs were streaming flat and straight across my face, and my lips felt numb. I meant to sound flip, and funny, but Raymond looked afraid of me all over again when I spoke, and I felt like slapping his flustered face. He and my father took keys out of their pockets at the same time, and seeing the effect this had on my father, Raymond stepped aside to let him open the door. They waved me in first, each opening a palm toward me.

I walked through the black foyer, holding my breath, and felt for the switch inside the kitchen. Turning it on, I saw an explosion of memory in light, and my hand jerked up to shield my eyes against the shock of the sudden and intimate brilliance. I took a step forward and let my breath out, then drew it in again.

My mother had moved nothing from this house to the next. Copper pots still hung on hooks in descending sizes by the stove; I opened a cupboard door and saw dishes, cups, and saucers stacked neatly in matching piles. It was the set I had helped my mother collect from the Grand Union over the years, taking a single piece home with a load of groceries every Saturday morning. The design was blue and white, pictures of people living at hearthside in Revolutionary times. I reached in to touch a plate and felt grit on my fingers, then snatched my hand away.

The spice rack under the window held jars of flakes and pepper, turned dusty by the sun. The plastic placemats with my crayoned daisy designs, which my mother once let go at a yard sale and then tracked down to buy back when I asked what happened to them, lay carefully around the table, as if a family might be settling in for supper soon. I always thought it was my mother's light I associated with this room, but now I saw that it was purely the arrangement of familiar things, reflected by glass and fluorescence in a certain consistent way, that made me love this place, though my mother was not here. Even the recipes remained.

"Jesus," I said. I was suddenly grateful for the presence of Raymond Dutille, because I knew I would never allow myself to cry in front of him. "She didn't tell me she left it all."

"That's a problem," Raymond said. "When we sell, someone will have to—" He hesitated.

"Get rid of all this crap," my father finished, helping him.

"Well, move it someplace else, anyway."

"I've been to her new house," I murmured. "I've slept there. I've eaten meals. But I never noticed what she didn't keep."

"Well, at least she left the bare necessities," my father said, stepping out of the pantry. He hugged two bottles to his wet chest, one whiskey and one wine.

"At least let's take off our coats first," I said. "What will Raymond think?" I dropped mine across the table, skewing the placemats, and cradled with my fingers the beer mug into which my father was sloshing some Bully Hill.

"I was going to offer that to our guest," my father said.

"Nothing for me, thanks." Raymond removed his raincoat carefully, and hung it across the back of an empty chair. He shook the umbrella out in the sink and opened it in a corner to dry. "Actually," he told us, "I'm a little worried about this snow. What it could do to the roads, I mean. Maybe we should get down to business, before it gets any worse." He turned away from the window in time to watch my father and me clinking drinks in a toast.

"To home sweet home," my father proposed.

"Bottoms up," I answered, and the two of us laughed.

"Nobody's been living here, right?" Raymond said in the silence that followed, as we let the shots settle. He ran a finger along the tops of ceramic baking cannisters in the figures of fat Dutch girls, leaving dusty imprints on their blond braid lids.

"She's kept up the mortgage, but I doubt there's any heat." My father still had his coat on. "I think I'll go down and take a look at the furnace. But I'd just as soon light the stove. That should be a big selling point, Ray—a working wood stove in the living room. Take a look."

"We're not going to be here that long, are we?" Raymond peered out the window again. It was getting dark, but we could see the snow against the sky, mounting, piling on our cars. "I mean, are you sure we need it?"

"I thought we'd spend the night here. Not *you*," my father said, laughing as he hurried to reassure Raymond, who looked dismayed. "But Francie, hon, you'll keep me company, won't you? Just one last night? And after we pull out of here tomorrow, you'll never hear me mention Seven Short Road again." His face was pink with the effort of hoping, and I agreed without wanting to, without even hearing myself give in. My father squeezed my elbow and went down to the basement, still wearing his coat and clumping heavily on each step.

Raymond and I looked at each other, and then away at other things in the room, the diagonal row of strawberry-shaped potholders hanging over the range, the hook by the telephone where penned messages that had been stuck there a year ago had yellowed, then disappeared. I knew I should be polite, but I had to bite back the automatic disdain I was used to treating him with. "You look pretty good," I told him finally, when he just sat there watching my drink go down. "I almost didn't recognize who you were."

"I don't always dress this well," he told me. "But like I said before, I thought it might be you." I blushed.

"What are you doing now?" he asked me quickly. "You don't still live around here. That I'd know."

"No. Boston."

"You go there for a job?"

"Not exactly. I got married."

"You like it there?" I knew he was imagining a place of light and excitement, a place the Francie Griffith he remembered could be expected to call home.

"Yes," I said, before the impulse to confess to someone could take hold, and shake from my bright lips the truth of what was happening to my life.

"What about you?" I said.

"Well, I got married, too." Raymond shrugged.

"You did? Who to?"

"Gwen Sperling."

"I don't remember her."

"You wouldn't." Raymond looked relieved and ashamed of it at the same time. "She was a grade behind us. And anyway, she wasn't in your crowd."

"I never had a *crowd*." I took a few drops of wine up my nose, snort-laughing as I spoke.

"What are you talking about? Of course you did." Raymond paused, looking down at the melted snowdrops between his feet. He seemed surprised by my denial.

"What do you call Andy Lutz and Cindy Fairchild and Lisa Prince?" His tongue touched the names with reverence, as if they were expensive sweets he had never been allowed.

"God," I said. I felt tingles of comfort in memory, the way I might if Raymond had reminded me of distant pleasant places I had visited as a child. "I haven't thought of them in ages. Are they still around?"

"Andy moved to Dayton. He married Wendy Spark. Cindy has two kids and works at Allstate. Lisa lives in town." He seemed embarrassed to be filling me in on the histories of my best friends.

Above the refrigerator, the clock clicked at the new hour. Raymond shifted, and I sensed in his movement a boldness that came from our privacy and my own silence, which implied he could go on. "Listen," he mumbled in a caught breath, down to the streaky floor.

"What?" Even though it was only Raymond Dutille, I was afraid of what I might hear. I poured more wine and some sloshed on the table, and I pressed my finger into the drop and sucked it.

"The day we got assigned to the pig together in biology," he began, blinking, "I thought, oh God, Francie *Griffith*." The worship in his voice sent heat to my face. "I was so nervous I thought I'd cut myself, or pass out from the fumes. But when you threw up in the hall, it made me feel better. Like you got sick *for* me." He looked up from the floor, and for the first time I saw that the eyes behind his glasses moved and changed light as he tried to find the right words.

"I figured you'd go to the nurse or something, and I wouldn't have to talk to you the whole rest of the class. I couldn't believe it when you came back. I was so close I could see your mouth trembling. I remember thinking, Francie Griffith *trembles*." He smiled and looked down. "Then I thought you'd just watch me do all the dissecting, but you wanted to take out the heart. You remember?"

"God, do I," I said, covering my eyes. I saw blood and muscle and my own fingers moving among veins that looked as though they might still be living, though they had never survived birth. "That was one hard-hearted piggy. It took forever."

"You should have seen your face." Now Raymond was laughing, and I realized that nothing about his laughter touched a place in my memory. "You had your tongue stuck out between your teeth, and it kept sliding around while you cut, so it looked like you were licking your chops. Like as soon as you finished slicing that pig heart, you'd put some salt on and dig in."

"Oh, God!" I slapped the table. "I didn't, did I? Why didn't you tell me? I remember that day. I forced myself to go through with it. I remember thinking, nothing could be worse than this. If you can get through this, you can get through anything." I began laughing with him, and then I was horrified to realize that I was not laughing anymore, but crying. By the time I knew it, it was too late, and I got up from the table, turned my back to Raymond and made a lunge for the paper towel rack above the sink. The sheet I ripped off was rough against my face, but I was grateful for the friction because it was something to feel. I wiped my skin raw and inhaled the rest of my tears.

Raymond had stood up and was trying to say something, but he was interrupted by a slam, my father shutting the door at the top of the basement and kicking off his shoes. "That mother *pipe*," he said, and when he came into the room, we saw that his forehead was bleeding. "She never got that light fixed. The damn pipe gets me every time." He picked up my scarf from the back of my chair and pressed it against his wound. Blood seeped through the yarn and beneath it, and he swore again as some dripped onto the linoleum. "Francie, hon, wipe that up for me, will you? Don't worry, Ray. We'll remove all traces of blood from the house before the new family moves in."

"I'm not worried about *that*." Raymond stood between the two of us, as if he didn't know who needed his help first. I bent down to scrub at the drops with my paper towel, so Raymond stepped closer to my father and looked at his forehead under the light. "That looks pretty bad, Mr. Griffith—can I call you Art? I think we should take you to the hospital or something."

"Nah. It'll dry up in no time. Besides, look at the mess out there, would you?" My father waved the bloody scarf toward the window, which was black with snow flecks whipping against the glass. "We'd all get killed on the way into Saint Pete's. I'll just lie down in the living room for a minute. Turn the tube on and warm up these bones. Francie, I'm afraid I'll have to ask you to start the fire in there, hon."

"Dad, are you sure? Maybe Raymond's right. Maybe someone should look at what happened." I stood by the sink, trying to focus, clenching in both fists the towel absorbing my tears and my father's blood.

"Nah. Just bring some wood in and start her up." Raymond followed the two of us into the next room, where my father switched on the TV and then eased himself down against the couch, lying as if it were a bed. The room was dark except for the flicker-light from the giant old set in the corner. "Whoops—forgot my snack," he said, and I got up from where I was crumpling newspapers to bring him his bottle. "Forgot my glass," he said then.

I got up again to go into the kitchen, and Raymond took over at the stove, setting the kindling down, poking the paper in, feeding the flame. "Good job, Ray," my father said. "What would you say to torching the joint for us? We'd cut you in on the deal." He took the glass I handed him and filled it with whiskey. "Thanks, hon. Do you think you could find me something funny on the tube, while you're up?"

Instead I went over to the TV set and turned the sound all the way down. "Are we going to do this real estate stuff today, or not?" I asked my father, who held a hand over his eyes to look at the screen, as if the sun were blinding his vision, or what he wanted to see was too far away. When he didn't respond, I turned the channel, found the old "Dick Van Dyke Show," and said, "Raymond, maybe you should come back in the morning. He's down for the count."

"I remember this one," my father said, pointing his glass

at the TV. "Mary Tyler Moore gets her toe stuck in the tub faucet." He began chuckling in anticipation, and I tried to yank my arm away even before I realized that Raymond had taken hold of it, lightly at the elbow.

"Francie," he said softly, and his voice held a measure of power between us that I hadn't realized I'd given up. When I didn't answer, he said, "Listen, he really should go to a doctor. Who knows how hard he was hit? I had a cousin once who when he was a little kid, got bashed by a shopping cart coming around the corner. He cracked his head on the shelf on his way down. Everybody thought he was okay at the time, but a few hours later he wouldn't wake up from a nap, and they found out he had a concussion. What's so funny?" I let myself collapse in the doorway between the two rooms.

"Oh, God," I said. "Only a relative of yours could get knocked out by a shopping cart. Was it an accident or premeditated? Or did it just start chasing him down the cereal aisle?" I banged the wall with my fist, to emphasize how funny I found it.

"He died," Raymond said.

I heard him, but I didn't stop laughing until later than I meant to. When I found my voice, I tried to make up for it. "I'm sorry," I told him. "I didn't mean to laugh. I didn't realize what you were saying." After a pause I asked him, "Which side was this cousin on?"

"I'm not talking about my goddam *cousin*." Raymond let his voice rise, but my father didn't seem to notice, from where he lay on the couch. "Let me take him to the hospital. I have four-wheel drive."

"No," I said, shaking my head, watching the wallpaper move. "I know him when he's like this, Raymond. We'd have to use a wheelbarrow to move him at this point."

"Will you let me go for somebody, then?"

"Nah. He's fine. Look, it's better already." I pointed across the room at my father's head, where the blood from the pipe gash had stopped sliding across his skin.

"Then what about you?" Raymond said. He let the circle of his fingers drop down on my arm to my wrist.

"What about me?"

"Will you come home with me? We have a guest bedroom. You could meet Gwen."

"What the hell would I want with your guest bedroom? We have our whole house." I gestured around us at the dark spaces. "Besides, somebody has to take care of him."

"But I'm afraid to leave you like this." Raymond was swallowing as he spoke. I looked at his eyes again, and a chill shook me when I saw that his glasses were dotted from the inside with tears.

I made myself laugh again. "Thanks anyway, partner." Then on a fresh bloom of inspiration I added, "I'd rather eat a pig's heart." I giggled, but stopped when it made me feel sick. I was trembling, holding myself steady against the counter with whitened hands.

Raymond went over and picked up his umbrella, snapping it shut. He put his coat on, shivering as his arms settled into wet sleeves. He took his glasses off and wiped them on the hem, and from his wallet he pulled out a business card. He approached me slowly, holding the card in front of him like a blind man testing the way.

"I'll go, but I want you to take this," he told me. When I didn't move, he reached down to pick my hand up, and closed my fingers around the cardboard. "Call me if you need anything. That's my home number there."

"Why would I want to call *you*?" I said, crumpling the card up and tossing it to the floor. I let myself slide down against the cabinet, where I hugged my knees. His shadow above me stole some of my breath. "God," I groaned, while he was still standing there, "Raymond Du*tille*."

I heard him start his car on the fourth try, and I pulled myself up to watch the headlights move slowly down the road through the snow. I took the wine bottle off the table, turned it around on its heel a few times until I saw that it was empty, then went into the living room to borrow some of my father's.

He was asleep with his mouth open. I picked up his glass and swallowed, hating the taste, and made a noise shuddering. My father closed his mouth and opened his eyes, and when he lifted his head, I saw that it was still bleeding.

"Dad, don't," I said, spilling the glass in my scramble to lay him back down. "It's opening up again."

"I blew it with Mom, you know," he said, letting his head fall back against the sofa cushion. With the comforter tucked under his chin, his skin looked translucent, and I could tell his eyes made no sense of what they were seeing. "I don't know what happened. I should give her a call."

"Stop," I said, and my voice blended with Hawkeye's on the TV.

"We lived on Eagle Street when you were born. You were a long labor, twenty-two hours. The doctor had to use a drug to make you come out." He tried to sit up again, but this time I caught him before he could flinch.

"I was watching TV in the waiting room," he went on, his breath warm against my arm. "It was the news, Vietnam. This one guy came back from the front with his chest blown up, and it was a miracle he could still breathe. When the nurse said I could see Mom, I thought I would make a little joke about the resemblance. You put her through the wringer, babe. I told her, 'you look like you just got back from the war.' "

I heard a heavy noise come out of my own throat, and my father appeared to smile. "That's just what she said! She made that same sound. I thought she might laugh a little, but she turned her back on me, and I heard her crying. They say that happens after babies, but I didn't know that then. The nurse made me leave. I didn't really meet you officially until the next day." His eyes roamed the walls.

"Remember?" he asked me. "We brought you home in a fruit basket. Left the nectarines on the bed."

I dropped his hand and aimed myself at the kitchen, where I picked up the phone and punched in my own number, my fingers fumbling, feeling fat. There was a buzzing sound, and then a series of rings at the other end. When Greg answered, he sounded farther away than Boston. I said, "Hon?"

"Where are you?" he asked me. His voice sounded empty, as if he had screamed it all out. I couldn't answer. "Are you all right?" he said.

I nodded and made a sound like yes. "Francie," he told me, "I can't come and get you this time." After a long moment, he hung up with the gentlest click.

I listened to the steady hum until it went haywire. The room vibrated in front of my eyes. On the floor, Raymond's business card lay with the sharp corners folded. I picked it up and dialed, and let it ring on this time across the hollow line.

The receiver was hot against my skin, and more solid than anything I could remember ever holding between my hands.

I would hang on until somebody answered.

From where I stood I could see my father's face, old and white, caved at the mouth, nerves slack, flesh rubbered around his eyes. He was fifty-three years old. The only time I had ever seen him cry was the day when I was eight and he came back from visiting his mother at the hospital, where she went to have tests to see how far the cancer had gone. He stood in the kitchen, with his hat in his hand, and cried that way, holding the hat, while my sister and my mother and I sat at the table, waiting. "It's got her," he said in a voice I didn't recognize, and my mother sent Jill and me out of the room. He had been young then, and his face was smooth under the tears.

My sister went upstairs. I watched "Bewitched" in the family room until my father came out of the kitchen and gave me a sip of his beer. We fell asleep on the couch together, and when I woke up my mother was sitting on the other side of the room, her face turned away from us, reading by light that wasn't bright enough, straining to see the page.

"Bedtime," I said, and my mother looked up surprised.

"Oh," she said, and a slow smile crossed her face as she stood to take my hand. We walked out of the dark room together and up the stairs in a bare yellow light. My mother was shaking her head, still smiling, when she tucked me in. She said, "I had no idea it had gotten so late."

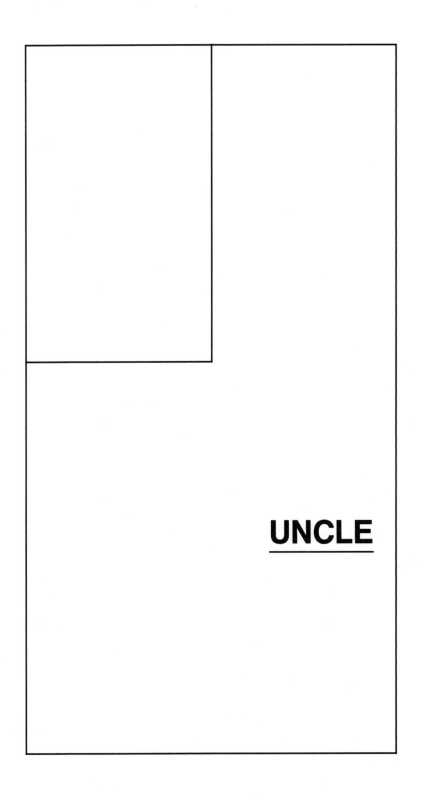

UNCLE

UNCLE

He was standing in a baby's bedroom, getting ready to go to church. If anybody had told him a year ago to expect either of these things about himself, Nate would have said they were nuts.

But everything was backwards these days. A junky bag lady had sworn and spit at him the other morning, instead of asking for money. Hell, here he was wearing the shoes he got married in, and a suit smelling of mothballs. He didn't know what it was that had changed in the world while he wasn't looking—would he find stars buried in the snow?—but he was trying to anticipate surprise now, so it couldn't grab him from behind.

He checked to make sure Vivien was still in the bathroom. Then he picked up one of the baby's toys, a stuffed rhino with a felt snout. He held it in the crook of his arm and rocked it, the way you did with babies, for a few seconds until chagrin made him smirk at the sight of himself in the gilt-framed mirror. He threw the rhino by its nose across the room, into the playpen, and shook his sleeves out to get rid of the toy's lint and the physical memory of the foolish embrace.

"Nate." The door from the bathroom opened into the nursery, and steam seeped out along with Vivien's curly head. "See if Judy left out some towels for us. I'm dripping, and it's freezing in here."

She was always freezing. *Thin blood*, he would tell her. *Nobody keeping me warm*, she would answer back.

The threat of her absence was in the air, like a tree's leaves turning before the rain.

But this weekend they were guests, and about to be godparents, so they spit out truce and suffered through it. Nate picked up the pile of terrycloth from the bureau, which had knobs made of bunny tails, and handed it to the white vapors.

A faint voice said something, but he couldn't make it out.

Vivien's suitcase sat open, next to their new niece's crib. He rummaged through it until he found the sandwich bag she wrapped her jewelry in, when she traveled. He picked up a pair of silver earrings, with short drop ovals, and untangled them from each other. Then he fit one through the hole in his left ear and admired the way it looked, glinting above the shoulder of his dark suit. Just right for church, he decided. Dressy, but not too loud. He hoped the priest would do a double-take, lose his place in the psalms.

"I'm ready," Vivien said, coming out of the bathroom clothed now, smelling like lemon cream rinse, wrapped in a polka-dot dress. "Oh, Nate, don't wear the earring. It might embarrass Judy and Robert. We're going to church, you know."

"I know," he told her. What did she think he was, retarded? "Nobody will care, Viv. Times have changed." He reached up to pat the nip of Seagram's sloshing gently behind his lapel, a supply in store, just in case. "Let's go already, before I choke inside this collar."

He held the bedroom door open so Vivien could go first. Her mouth tightened at the polite gesture she didn't expect. "That must be something your tootsie taught you," she said, but he didn't bother to answer her. The fact that she could think he was still seeing Bonnie (though Vivien had never wanted to know her name) made him almost want to go back on his promise.

What if he did call her up this weekend, long-distance,

as long as Vivien expected nothing more of him? What did he have to lose?

He would have to make it collect, though. Lately, he found himself running out of change.

On the way to the church Nate and Vivien sat in the back seat with the baby between them, strapped in her car seat and wrapped like a fragile ornament in her white blanket. "You can see why we have to move," Robert said over his shoulder, as he drove. "How this town is going down the tubes." With the hand by the window he pointed out the housing development being built in what had clearly been, once, a Christmas tree field, raised on a hill by the side of the road. Half the houses were already up; the others were frame skeletons that had been abandoned, for Sunday, to stand in the mud. A sign in front of the field said *Pine Village* though there were only a few pines left, scattered in a broken circle around the lot. They looked forlorn, like children too far apart from one another who still struggle to hold hands.

"Yuck," Vivien said.

"I kind of like them." Nate turned to look back through the rear windshield. "I bet even we could afford something like that."

"Don't let the crappy structures fool you. Those houses are going for almost as much as ours." Robert's face looked stern; he had a professor's countenance even on his days off. "There's something weird about those kinds of developments. The people are well enough off to buy a house, but they have trailer mentalities. It's like it preselects for a lower class that has nothing to do with how much money they have."

"I grew up in a place like that," Nate said. He knew this would cause a silent rumble through the car, and it was one of the reasons he said it. In the front seat Robert and Judy looked at each other, and next to him, over the baby's head, Vivien looked out her window at the snow. "But I guess that just proves your point, doesn't it?" He closed his eyes against the sun coming in, and swallowed hard to settle the pitch in his stomach. Something was murmured between the two sisters.

When he opened his eyes again, they had arrived at the church. Three other babies were to be christened along with Lesley Anne, and four parents for each—two real ones and two gods. Nate sat between Judy and Vivien, and tried to make his mind blank as the minister floated down the aisle.

He began mending a staircase in his head, trimming boards and pounding nails, but he didn't get very far before he realized that what he was building was Bonnie, starting at the top with her fresh wild hair, almost feeling it on his skin as sweat broke on his hands and he rubbed them on the top of his suit pants. Next to him, Vivien smiled a little sadly and reached over to touch the band on his finger; the last time they had been in church together, she had put it there.

He jerked his hand away, and she looked pissed. "You gave me a shock," he whispered, sliding his pant leg against her stockinged calf, to make up for it.

They were all called forward to the altar. During the ceremony, Nate focused on the woman standing across from him, holding a baby with red ears. At first he thought the woman was making a face at him, but it was only a nervous movement with her nose. The minister told the parents to make known their wishes for the children. "We ask for God's guidance in shaping our daughter's soul, and the strength to help her be an instrument of God's mercy," Judy said, when her turn came.

They had rehearsed it the night before, during dinner. At the time, Nate had been pouring himself more wine in the kitchen, and he had mimicked the words to himself, moving his lips in his sister-in-law's mincing, prideful way. When he came back into the dining room, they all paused in their talk as if he were a stranger about to ask directions. He would have sworn that none of them recognized him in that moment, not even his wife.

The people in the congregation recited something after

Judy, and Nate started to whisper a question to Vivien about how they knew what to say, but she wouldn't listen, and she put a bitten fingernail to her lips.

Bonnie's nails were always long and smooth, and painted some color that reminded him of candy. She spoke in questions: *Do you like this nightie? How does Mexican strike you for tonight?* Nate came to love being asked, because it meant she would then listen for his response. The rise of a voice putting out a question, and the falling inflection of another voice answering, was like making love, he thought—going up and coming down again, that circle it took two people to complete.

Since he had known Bonnie, he tried to use the same language with Vivien. *What's in your head at this very second?* he said to her on an instinct once, a few months ago. They were sitting on the porch, drinking beer and waiting for Bill Dodd to come and snake out the toilet. It was a summer night, and when she turned to look at him her face was framed by pink sky, and against the rich pain of its beauty, which he felt down to his gut, he saw surprise and then suspicion shade her hopeful eyes. *Nothing*, she said, getting up to go into the house.

At the altar, the parents held the babies up over their heads, and when his brother-in-law, Robert, lifted Lesley Anne into the air and showed the dark startled face out to the crowd, Nate saw that Vivien was biting back tears. This scared him, so he tried repairing something in his mind again—this time a simple cabinet with a broken door—until the ceremony was over. They sat down as everyone smiled at the babies, and immediately Lesley Anne began to whine. Judy tried to pat her into silence, but the sounds only grew. Another mother carried her son out of the pew and through the front doors of the sanctuary, and Judy began to follow. Nate reached up to pull her back.

"I'll go," he said, feeling sweat spread beneath his pits.

His sister-in-law hesitated, then placed the baby against his chest. "Be careful," she whispered.

He carried Lesley Anne out to the sunshine, and her

head lolled back against his lapel as the sudden light stabbed at her eyes. He moved out beyond the shadow of the church's roof and watched flies swarm around something dead in the rusted rail tracks across the road. When the branches blew, he could see through them to a grocery store with a sign that said WARRENTON PUBIC MARKET— someone had pulled off the L in the second word—behind the one-hour photo hut at the bottom of the hill.

For a moment the sight of the sign caught Nate's breath. In high school, on a date once, he had lost control of his father's Chevy and driven unintentionally into the front of a Purity Supreme, sending Dawn Spinosa through the windshield. He had only been nicked by slivers, but Dawn needed stitches across her whole forehead. When he saw her later in the year, it looked as if the skin had been zipped up to keep her brains inside.

But that was a long time ago, and she grew bangs to compensate. Besides, this was a different store chain. Nate shifted the baby against his shoulder, thinking about Bonnie. Was that a phone booth he saw over there, in front of the market? He could go to a phone booth, if he wanted to; it wasn't against the law. Going to a phone booth didn't mean you were going to call. He began lifting his feet over the rise of the ancient tracks.

Behind him the church was quiet, no sign of anyone leaving, no bells letting out the lambs. When he got to the booth, he shook the coins from his pocket into his palm and saw that he had just enough to make the connection. Instead of thrilling him, this made him nervous, and he squinted at the money hoping he'd see that something was Canadian and wouldn't work in the machine. When this didn't happen, he took a step toward the phone, then stopped, and let the coins slide back down the pocket on his leg. He was stuck in one of those long moments of decision, waiting for a sign from God to make up his mind for him.

He walked over to the store window. Through the glass, in the checkout line, he saw a man about his own age, wearing a camel-hair coat and laying a pie crust and Saran Wrap and Huggies on the counter. A small boy sat in the front of the shopping cart, facing his father, kicking his Weeboks into the air. As the cashier pushed their things through, the father reached into a pocket of his coat, took out a comb and ran it gently through his son's blond-sheeted hair, three times to each side; then, leaning back to get a better view, he reached over again and pulled the comb once down across the boy's straight bangs.

The boy sat patiently, swinging his shoes without speaking, examining the things inside the billfold his father had handed him. The way the father cocked his head to the side, considering what he had done before putting the comb back into his pocket, reminded Nate of movies he had seen about artists, the way they would brush a stroke of paint on the canvas and then step back to admire what they had created, and figure out how they might still improve it.

"Jesus," Nate said. He looked sideways at the baby drooling white stuff on his shoulder. He had forgotten what it was, cutting into the muscle above his sleeve. He wiped the goo off with the hem of Lesley Anne's christening dress and told her she shouldn't go slobbering all over married men. Though of course she couldn't understand what he was saying, his niece opened her red mouth and laughed.

The camel-coated man was wheeling his cart out of the store. He stopped short as he approached where Nate was standing, and let a wheel spin away from him. "Damn," the man said. "I just remembered what I forgot." When he saw Nate he asked, "Look, could you watch him for a minute?"

"I have to get back to—" but Nate realized he was embarrassed to say "*church*," so he just nodded and said, "Okay, but you better hurry."

The man turned in a rush toward the entrance. "Thanks. She's a doll," he said, bobbing his head at Lesley Anne, whose blanket had fallen away from her dress. Nate looked down and pulled the blanket back around the little body, as if afraid of being caught naked himself. The father disappeared into the store.

"Look," the blond boy said to Nate, reaching into the grocery bag nearest him and pulling out a billfold from behind a box of Wheat Thins.

"Shit," Nate said. The father was too far away to be called back with a shout.

A young woman was walking by. "What's the matter?" she said. She had just come out of the store and was watching Nate with a look he recognized from his own reflection, danger inside a smile. She was tucking a pack of cigarettes into the middle pocket of her sweatshirt, where her hands would normally go. The pouch looked stuffed, and he caught a glimpse of packaged soup sticking out of one side, and on the other side a small block of Velveeta.

Because of the sweatshirt it was hard to tell her shape, but Nate knew from the slender jeaned legs jutting down beneath that it was probably pretty good, tight muscles in the calf, and the skin there maybe still browned by the last tan of summer. Loose black hair fell on the sweatshirt's shoulders, and her eyes were dark and deep, like slits of intelligent velvet.

"Anything I can help you with?" she said to Nate, her smile reaching high in her face, her gaze moving toward his earring with approval and intrigue.

"Ah," Nate said. He was distracted by the sounds of the two children—the boy was poking at Lesley Anne's booty— and by the woman's sudden beauty. "This wallet—I mean—" His mind was not making the connections he needed, and then all he could do was laugh.

The woman smiled, too. "I didn't mean to confuse you right off the bat," she said, taking a step closer, tapping her high red sneaker on the curbstone. Her face cast a darting shadow in the small space between their feet. "Let's try another one. What's the baby's name?"

"Lesley Anne." He couldn't remember the last time he had given what he knew was the right answer; he had forgotten how good it felt.

"She's adorable."

"Yeah."

"She looks just like you." He laughed again, until he realized she hadn't meant it as a joke. "How about the boy?" she said then.

"What about him?" The kid was opening a box of whole wheat spaghetti. He took some sticks out and began breaking them over the cart.

"Are you going to just let him do that?" The woman seemed amused.

"Of course not," Nate said, taking the box from the boy, who gave a short shriek. "Stop that, Kenneth." Kenneth was the name of Judy and Robert's terrier, who also had blond hair.

"Well, they sound very classy." The woman ripped the cellophane off her cigarettes and stuck one between her lips. "Want one?"

"I gave them up." This was an abrupt lie; he could feel his own hard pack in the pocket against his thigh. But the person she thought he was would never have taken up cigarettes, or would have quit them years ago in favor of jogging and Nautilus. "Thanks, though." His tongue itched for a drag, and when she drew in smoke he could feel it in his own breath. They exhaled together.

"I know they're supposed to be bad for you. But I look at it this way. I say, I could get hit by a train tomorrow, I might as well die with a good taste in my mouth. You know?" She spoke in an accent familiar to Nate. Tough girls. They made him tingle.

"I used to smoke. Don't get me wrong. It's just that my wife is allergic." He shifted Lesley Anne, feeling further inspired. "Besides, it's bad for children. Second-hand smoke, they call it. You might as well just stick a Lucky in their mouths."

"Well, I guess you would know." The woman smoked with a small sucking noise, and the boy he had named Kenneth began searching through bags for more food to play with. Nate kept his eyes on the door behind the woman, watching for the real father to come out and end this game. The woman made a movement toward him, and he stepped back, wondering where this impulse to retreat had come from; but she was only smoothing Lesley Anne's hair down behind her ears.

"Does she take after you or your wife?" the woman asked.

"I guess me," Nate said, smiling, narrowing his eyes and hoping they gave off a gleam, so she would know how lucky his wife was.

"You happen to have a picture, by any chance?"

"Of what?"

"Your wife." She shrugged. "I mean, for comparison sake. I was just wondering." She nodded toward the billfold in the seat next to the boy. Nate picked it up, feeling its leather heat prick his fingers.

"I'm not the type who usually carries pictures," he said, in case, but as he opened the billfold, a plastic accordion photo jacket slipped from behind the father's American Express. Nate drew it out gingerly; the top photo was one of the boy, taken recently, and on the flip side was a woman with long hair nudging the shoulders of a blue sweater, a pearl necklace stringing the collar. It looked like a yearbook picture, except that the mouth and eyes carried fewer creases than Dawn Spinosa had by high school already fretted into her skin.

"Here," he said, offering the picture as if it were a membership pass.

The woman squinted at the photo. "What's her name?"

"Vivien." The true answer fell out of his mouth before he could think to invent another.

"And how did you end up with each other?" The woman flipped her cigarette, still burning, into the dumpster. Nate flinched invisibly, expecting something to explode, but nothing happened.

"You mean how did we meet?"

"That's not the same thing."

He felt the jump beneath his ribs that always came when

Vivien told him he was wrong about something, or when he knew he had screwed up. "Well," he said, not sure what she was asking. "We used to work at the movies together. I was an usher and she was the concession girl." The woman was looking at him with her face tilted, as if she cared what he was saying. He felt himself blush and he had to move his eyes away from hers.

"It's not like we knew each other before that—she was in college," he went on. "She was putting herself through. I was just this schmuck with a truck, fixing things for people. I still am." Too late, he realized he was telling his own story, not some other guy's, not the story of a man who would ever come to stand in front of a supermarket with two children and bags filled with a supply of food for a family. But the woman's face, still lifted toward him, still inviting him to speak, pulled the words from him even as he told himself to shut up.

"A lot of nights, it was just the two of us working. We'd talk while the movie was going on. She wouldn't have hung out with me if she had a choice, but she didn't, so she did. If you get what I'm saying." Nate tried to laugh.

"She tell you that?" the woman said.

"Well, no." It was getting chilly. He held the baby closer as her eyes blinked against the breeze. "One night a bunch of popcorn fell all over the floor," he said without realizing he was going to, and the woman, who had glanced down at her watch, looked up abruptly, as if he had just told her the beginning of a joke that took her by surprise.

"Not already *popped*," he clarified, seeing she was trying to picture it. "I mean the kernels. She missed the machine. I could have sworn she spilled it on purpose. She asked me to help her sweep it up, and when we got down on the floor, I could tell she wanted to kiss me." His voice cracked on the word *"kiss"*; he hardly ever said it.

"Did she? Kiss you?" The woman smiled again, her eyes drawing lines as her lips pursed on a new cigarette.

"Well, no. I was too nervous. I kept talking, like a jerk."
Like I am now, he thought—but he didn't want to stop until

he was finished. He recognized this moment as one of those few he had always imagined his future to hold in store for him, when forced by desperation or opportunity he was going to say something he had not known he knew, and it would be truer than anything he had ever said before.

"So there we were squatting down around all this popcorn, and I started to laugh, thinking how that used to be our punishment, when I was a kid—my mother would spread popcorn kernels or sometimes beans in the kitchen corner, and make us kneel down on it, for however long, depending on what we did to piss her off." Nate was careful not to let the woman know he was looking at her, though he was—to see if there was anything in her face like what he had seen on Vivien's that night.

But the woman smiled. "Ha," she said. "That's a new one. A waste of good popcorn, though. Or did it taste better after that?"

Nate looked at her straight on, and for the first time he saw the depression in her forehead made by the sad squeeze of her brow. "I used to laugh at it, too," he told her. "I just assumed it was funny. But Vivien told me it wasn't." He paused and closed his eyes, smelling butter and Prell, the old scents of her sympathy.

"Then she did kiss me, right there on the floor. We were leaning against the candy case, and I could feel the popcorn underneath. When we stopped, because the movie was letting out, she had all these yellow teeth in her hair." He could tell the woman thought he was nuts, or she didn't believe him. But—and this was a gift he would never have guessed at—he didn't care.

"That ever happen to you?" he asked her. "Like with me and popcorn. Something you always hated turns into something you can love?"

She was about to give some smart-ass answer when Nate saw, behind her, the man in the camel coat on his way out of the store. "I have to go now," he said to the woman. Lesley Anne sneezed.

At the same moment, as he was sprayed by the thin film

of baby snot and moved to wipe his cheek, he felt the cart jammed hard against his body, and the woman bolted behind him, away from the store through the back of the parking lot, up the side street toward the row of new houses on the hill. Nate steadied the blond boy, who had fallen forward in the shove's force, and even before he could bring the cart to a rest, he knew that the billfold was gone. The boy cried as his father came out of the store and hurried over. "Did I leave my—" the father said, but Nate was already moving.

"She stole it. I'll get it back," he called over his shoulder, instinctively pressing Lesley Anne against his chest, with his big hand holding her head to his body close and careful, like a football. She seemed to sense in his flight a need for her cooperation, because she became silent, and still, making herself light inside his clutch. They were a single runner as he pushed up the hill. He felt the tail of his suit jacket flapping behind him in the breeze, and heard his stiff black loafers as they made squeaking noises on the pavement.

He had seen her run in the direction of the house set farthest apart from the others, raised up on cement blocks like a cat on its haunches, preparing to pounce. Without pausing to plan, he went straight to the flimsy door and pulled it open, and the hinge fell off its spring and let the door fall with a clunk to the ground. Glass shattered around his shoes. The noise made Lesley Anne flinch inside her blanket, but she kept quiet, making mouth movements without sound.

It was dark inside the kitchen. He had to blink a moment before his eyes adjusted to the dusty sunlight sifting in through a small window above the sink. Now that he had stopped chasing, he didn't know what to do. There was a movement behind him, and then the woman stepped out of the shadows.

"Who gave you the right to come in here?" she said, her voice shrilly metallic as she moved to inspect the shards. "Look what you did to my door. I'm going to sue, unless you get out of here now." She had taken off the sweatshirt, and she wore a black sweater over her jeans. Her cheeks looked flamed.

"I came to get the wallet," Nate said.

"No wallets here," she answered, laughing a little, speaking more calmly now.

"Trish, hon, what's going on?"

Nate blinked again and then saw the man sitting at the table in the back of the room. He held the wallet open in front of him, and was spreading its contents out around the remains of a hero sandwich. He pulled out bills, some photographs, a spare key. The man was also calm, his bare feet remaining still and flat on the carpet square that held the table steady. He looked at Nate and the baby with hurt bewilderment, as if they had interrupted something they knew to be important.

"Look, that's it." Nate felt a shock, trying to remember how he had gotten here, how he had moved so swiftly from the warm sanctuary of the church to this sour, battered room where his eyes ached from straining through the dark. "Just give it back and we'll forget about it, okay?"

The woman made a slow movement toward him. She reached up to finger the bottom of his earring, and sighed as if the contact had given her pleasure. "Tell you what," she proposed, from deep in her throat, "we'll give you back your precious pictures, and then you get out of here. Sound good?" She was so close he could smell the scent of flower lotion across her chest. The space between the two of them felt charged, and the baby nearly squirmed out of Nate's arms and fell down into it.

"I want it all back," he said, daring to take a step into the house and back toward the man who held the money.

"Get out before I hurt you," the woman warned.

"She means it, too," the man said from behind her, where he was waving bills in the air.

"Yeah, right. Sure she does." Nate could have taken the whole of her thin brown neck inside one hand, and snapped it clean across the middle. But in an instant, as if she had sensed this conclusion in him, she darted swiftly to the floor behind him and back upright again, holding a piece of glass above her head.

"Hey, watch it, Trisha, you'll cut yourself," the man said, still not moving from his seat.

Nate saw the glass glinting as it flashed in the sunlight, and took back the step he had claimed. "Okay," he said slowly, in the voice he used to talk to old people and foreigners. "I'm leaving. Just let us go, okay?"

The woman brought the glass higher. "The hell I will," she said, and he saw that the arm was moving even as he protested. She came closer toward him with a hop, like a wild dance step, and before he had the sense to duck she sliced the air in front of his face, and stroked his cheek with a sharp edge. The skin felt hot, stung, and Nate's voice caught in his throat on a curse. His hand went up and touched a warm streak of wetness, and taking it away he saw blood on his fingers, and blood smeared in the baby's white dress.

"Jesus, Trish," the man said, finally getting up, padding thickly toward her in his bare feet. She had raised the glass again and seemed about to swing a second time, but he caught her wrist behind her head and held it there, jerking it in his grip. "Can't you see the guy's got a baby, for Christ's sake?" The man turned to Nate, still holding the woman back, and said, "Hurry up, get out of here," but Nate had already seen that he was saved, and was on his way out the door before the man could finish sending him.

He stumbled down the hill, awkward with his bundle, and when he looked back and saw that no one had followed him, he stopped by a tree, set Lesley Anne down by the trunk, and put his hands to his face again. The cut was still bleeding, but less steadily; he pulled out one of the baby's layers, balled it up and held it tightly against his skin. Lesley Anne began to cry as he took the warmth of the blanket and of his own body away from her, and he picked her up again with one arm, tucking her inside his jacket flap like something he hoped to smuggle. Then he stood and looked around him, forgetting that he was in a place he didn't know.

Beyond the railroad tracks, people were filing out of the church and across its frosted lawn as the sound of steeple bells skittered through the air. He saw clumps of thin bodies in fancy clothes, gathering for family photographs and Sunday chatter. At the entrance, he could make out Vivien and then Judy as she gestured nervously to the minister, who bent forward with a hand behind his ear, as if he couldn't take in all that she was saying. Robert was walking with grim posture around the back of the church, bending to peer under bushes and boards.

"Shit," Nate said. He began to run toward the tracks, trying to shout, but he knew he was just far enough away that they wouldn't hear him.

"Hey! Right there." A voice came up behind Nate in the road, and he slowed down as a police car pulled alongside and cut off his path. The father from the supermarket got out with the cop, and together they came toward him. Nate could see the blond kid in the back seat, sucking a yogurt popsicle.

"I have to get this baby back to that church," Nate told them before they could say anything, as if they had appeared by magic to solve his problem. "They don't know where she is, and they're all worried."

"That right?" the cop said. He looked warily at the earring dangling above Nate's shoulder, and peered forward at the blood among Lesley Anne's clothes. "Hey, she hurt?"

"No. It's from me," Nate said, pointing to his cheek.

The cop leaned back on his heels, looking relieved. "Well, maybe you better give her over to us, then. Do you know her name? Who she belongs to?"

"Of course," Nate said. "This is my niece and my god-daughter, Lesley Anne."

The cop's eyes narrowed in doubt as he looked down at the baby, as if he expected her to comment on the truthfulness of Nate's story. "This the guy that stole your wallet?" he said to the other man.

"I don't know. I never saw him take it, but they might have been in on it together." The man looked as if he might be inclined to shake Nate's hand, but wondered if he should kick him instead.

"*I* didn't steal anything." Nate felt the blood soaking through the cloth on his face. "This crazy girl up the hill took his billfold, and I was trying to get it back. Jesus." His gut went faint. "Look, can't you see I'm bleeding? Think I did this to myself? Just take me to the church and then we'll worry about the wallet, okay?" He went to the police car and got in the back seat on the other side of the boy, holding Lesley Anne in his lap.

The cop looked startled at being told what to do, but he followed hastily, directing the boy's father back into the car. The boy looked at the cloth on Nate's face, then down at the frozen pop in his hand, and lifted it over to hold the cold ice mass against the swelling. Nate pulled back sharply at the sudden touch, but then pressed the ice closer as the pain began to numb. They sped off down the road and took the railroad crossing bumpily, scattering pebbles and dirt.

When they drove up in front of the church, Judy saw them first and ran toward the car stiffening, like somebody afraid to see what it was she was being pulled toward against her will. Nate got out of the police car before it had rolled to a stop, and she pitched herself forward at him.

"You idiot!" she shrieked. "Where did you go with her?" She went to take the baby from him; when she saw the blood on the christening dress her hands jerked back for an instant, then reached out again as she gasped in a huge moan of air. "What the hell did you do to her, you stupid fuck?" Robert had come to his wife's side, and Vivien followed. When she saw Nate's injured face, she gave out a startled sound, but she stopped short before touching him.

"It's my blood, not hers," Nate told them all. He started to add, "I didn't do anything wrong," but then he remembered that this wasn't the truth, and that they wouldn't believe him anyway.

"Do you know this man?" the cop said to Judy.

"Yes," Judy said.

"Do you want to press charges?" Nate could feel that the cop wanted her to say *yes* again, but Judy shook her head.

"Of course not. He's family," she said. When she had pulled Lesley Anne free of the blankets and seen the white skin unbroken beneath the blood, she added, "He's just dumb, not a criminal."

Robert touched his wife's elbow, but it was too late. Nate looked down at the ground and saw red flecks in the dirty snow. The blood was starting to seep.

"Well, we still have the wallet business to clear up," the cop said.

"Ever hear of a hospital?" Nate pulled the blanket away from his cheek, letting them all see the wound. "Do you think it would be asking too much to get me some help?"

Even the cop winced when he saw it. Judy and Robert looked at Nate for a minute, then looked away, and began walking to their own car, hugging the baby between them. Vivien stood where she had been watching from, still without moving.

"I guess we should get that taken care of," the cop told Nate. "Come on."

"What about my money?" The man in the camel-hair coat tramped up behind them on the hard crust. In the car, his son was using the stick from his yogurt bar to shoot at the people standing outside the church.

"I'll tell you where to find her. You can get your own face destroyed." Nate paused by the side of the car, waiting to see what Vivien would do. He waited for her to turn her back, to kick bloody ice chips in his direction, to drop her eyes without confessing that she knew him. Members of the congregation were watching from the dead lawn, closed in safe circles, murmuring. He shut his eyes and prepared himself for the attack.

Vivien came over. He felt her standing before him and he opened his eyes.

"It hurts, doesn't it?" she asked, reaching up slowly to catch his blood. When it began to drip from her cupped palms she knelt to clean them, and when she had finished he lifted her cold hands from the cold snow and began to rub the feeling back into them.

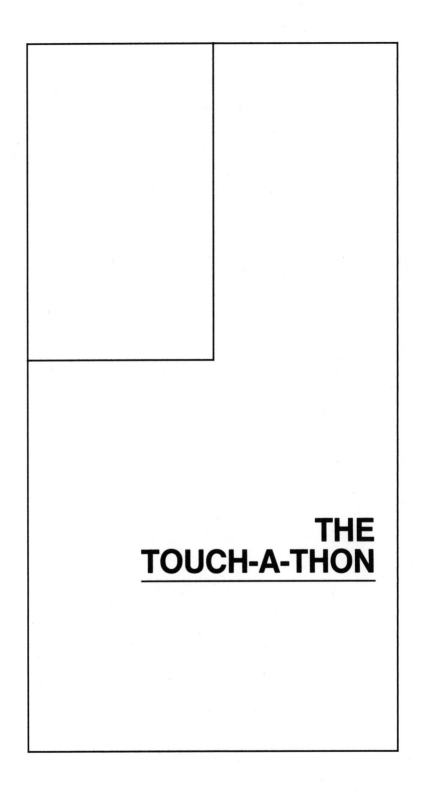

THE
TOUCH-A-THON

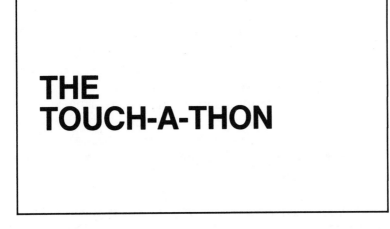

THE
TOUCH-A-THON

When George and Ginny stepped into the house out of the pouring rain, grocery bags turning soggy against their coats, their daughters were waiting to throw grenades.

"Look what *time* it is," Cara accused them. Then her impatience spread slowly into horror. "You didn't wear that—*thing*—into the actual supermarket, did you, Mom?" she asked, being the oldest at fifteen, and in charge of such investigations.

Ginny pulled off the rain bonnet she got at the Curly Cue the last time she had her hair trimmed. "I most certainly did," she said, folding the wet plastic along its design of brass-colored daisies. "It was admired greatly, and I told everyone it was a Christmas gift from my daughters, who fight over the privilege to borrow it on rainy school days."

But Diane would not be humored. "We're going to be *late*," she insisted, pushing the sleeves of her sweatshirt up over her elbows. "I told Melanie we'd pick her up at twelve-*thirty*." Diane was thirteen, their younger, more nervous child. George looked at the thin face, at the large eyes blinking behind glasses that had been taped together at the hinge, and knew that in another minute she would be crying.

"I'll take them," he said to Ginny. "Come on, you guys."

"Let's *go*," Diane said tightly. George followed his girls out to the car and climbed alone into the front seat. He tried to remember when this had happened, when Cara

and Diane had stopped fighting over the seat next to him
and chosen instead to share the back, but the date of this
betrayal eluded him. He used to enjoy having his daughters
beside him as he drove, used to love as he steered catching a small face upturned and smiling at him faithfully. Now
all he got were the tops of their heads, or sometimes a
horizontal strip of eerily empty eyes, in his rearview mirror.

"Do you have to wear all that gunk?" he said over his
shoulder to Cara.

"What?"

"On your eyes. And your nails," he told her. Her eyelids
were smeared with a purple chalk, and her fingers flashed
vermilion as she gestured.

"Yes, I do," she answered. "And it's not gunk, everybody
wears it, it's no big *deal*."

"It really isn't," Diane said loyally.

He knew to shut up about it then. "What movie are you
going to see?" he asked, but they must not have heard
him. He listened to talk of hunks and jocks and burnouts as
he drove, wetly, the familiar streets to Melanie's house. It
was a trip he made at least once a week. In the driveway,
they waited until a tall girl, taller than either of his daughters,
sauntered out in the prickling rain, a sweater draped over
one arm.

"God God *God*," Melanie said, also shunning the front,
falling into the back seat next to Diane. She took a comb
out of her back pocket and wielded it expertly, her head
flipped forward so that her long hair fell in her lap. "They
make you take a jacket for a little *rain*. Like it's *December*
or something."

"Really," Cara agreed. From Melanie's house it was a
matter of minutes to the CineMaxx, and George drove as
fast as he could without skidding, the windshield wipers
making soft rubber whines across the distant, fretful voices.
He turned on the radio and in the same motion turned it off
again, remembering that the station he kept it tuned to, for
the Oldies Hour every morning, would embarrass his
daughters. He pushed in the cigarette lighter and pulled it

out again, remembering that smoke made Melanie want to puke. He opened his window slightly, letting the damp air chill the side of his cheek, but there was a chorus of protest behind him and he rolled it up again, haste making him spastic.

"It's just that it frizzes out the perm, Dad," Diane said, and he was touched by her solicitude in bothering to explain.

They were in front of the theater now, in a line of cars driven by other parents, kids spilling out into the parking lot and through the dark, sinister entrance to the lobby. Diane and Cara got out and Melanie followed, now holding her sweater like a pup tent above her coiffure. "Mr. Martin will pick us up after," Cara shouted.

"What time?" George demanded wildly, rain poking his face through the open window.

"Three-thirty," Melanie answered calmly. She remained close to the car, superior to the rain, daring the wetness to touch her, and George felt a shock of dismay at her fragrant allure. In a year she would be somebody's seducer.

"If he remembers," Melanie added, calling back over her shoulder as the rain came harder and she finally ran. Then they were gone, clapped safe and dry inside the building, and George was alone with his wet face. He pulled into an empty parking slot to wipe his glasses, then saw that behind him a car was waiting to take the space, another father sitting with his forehead pressed in weariness against a drop-streamed window. George gave a comradely wave and pulled out to let the other guy park. He rolled through the lot, knowing he did not want to go straight home, where he was certain to be awaited by jobs that needed doing; the radiator in the girls' bedroom was making "like these weird clinking sounds, Dad," and the trash compactor had been spitting up crushed soup cans and melon rinds. Ginny would be folding the laundry on the kitchen table, making wool snowballs from pairs of socks, mixing up the girls' underwear with her own. The rain would depress the dog.

George got to the end of the parking lot, and when the light at the intersection turned green he let the steering wheel slide left instead of right, away from the direction of his own neighborhood. On the highway he saw a sign for CROSSROADS SHOPPERS PARK, in the next town over, and he lingered in the lane until he was forced to turn off at the exit. He would go to the mall, he realized, and dawdle anonymously among the ranks of idle browsers. The thought of straying to a new place cheered him.

It was dry inside the mall, and the raw yellow sheen of stores bounced around him in a comforting glow. He walked through Sears, touching the handles of spades and hammers, as if he might consider buying one, as if gardens or bookshelves might actually one day take shape beneath his fingers. He brushed by negligees and raincoats, and thought about buying his daughters matching pink rain slickers, until he remembered the elegant and unexpected contours of the London Fog he'd seen Melanie wearing one night when he'd driven them all to a party. The slickers would probably be laughed at, or, which would be worse, pitied; he passed by them without stopping.

He moved forward into the hum of canned music and the intimacy of half-heard conversations. "You get rid of one and the others are just hanging there," one woman was telling another as George cleaved a path between them, moving the opposite way. Outside Sears the mall widened, making four square walls around a fountain spraying blue. He felt a couple of pennies in his pocket, and walking by he let them drop into the water. They joined the other round brown glints on the scarred pool bottom, and he realized, too late, that he'd forgotten to make wishes.

He walked past bookstores and shoe stores and a cafeteria, where macaroni florentine was the Feature Du Jour. He considered new hardcovers, suede dress boots, and the macaroni aromas. In the center of the mall, he saw that a crowd of people had gathered in a circle, near a spot like the one where he had stood in many Christmas seasons, waiting to usher his daughters into Santa's green tin tree. He imagined that the current attraction must be a caricaturist or a traveling petting zoo.

He made his way through the people, gently, and found himself standing beside a yellow cordon, which wound around a raised square platform the size of a garage. TOUCH YOUR WAY TO TREASURE! proclaimed a large banner stretched across the top. Below the banner was a small handwritten scoreboard that read HOUR: 7, the number stuck on with Velcro for easy replacement. In the middle of the square space was a ten-foot-high wooden bar and beam, resembling a gallows, with hundreds of cash bills hanging from the top, by string, in bunches of different lengths.

Five people, three women and two men, stood next to this structure, each with an arm lifted high in the air. Their fingers touched dangling packets of dollar bills, bound at the middles by red ribbon. One of the women had on a blouse that had come untucked, and a section of her bare stomach was exposed to the side of the crowd George stood in. One of the men had sweat stains the size of cantaloupes under his arms. George averted his eyes from these embarrassing displays, then looked around for a camera, thinking it all must be some kind of television gimmick. But he saw none, and concluded with sad surprise that the scene he had stumbled into was something out of real life.

"Yes, ladies and gentlemen! It's the ultimate money giveaway of the year!" George looked up, startled by the sudden noise, and saw a short man in an umber-colored suit speaking to the crowd through a megaphone. He was standing on an overturned milk crate at the edge of the platform.

"You are witnessing the first annual Lady Love Cash Touch-A-Thon, brought to you by Lady Love Incorporated, makers of fine skin care and cosmetic products! Twelve entrants began our contest at six A.M. this morning, and all but five have dropped out of the picture. One of these fine folks will walk away with all this money—five C-notes, yes that's five hundred greenbacks ladies and gentlemen—in their lucky little fists. All that contestant has to do is remain in contact with the money, with one arm suspended in the air, longer than anybody else. And remember, there are *no strings attached.* Well, not many, anyway. A ha ha ha." The man pointed at the threads holding the bills to the wooden crossbar above his head.

"Who will be our most talented toucher? Lady Love, sponsor of this unique extravaganza, urges you to salute our hardy competitors." He stuck the megaphone under his umber armpit and began to clap, and George joined in the staccato ripple stammering through the crowd. The five contestants smiled bleakly at the applause, and George was reminded of his daughters' earliest ballet recitals at Miss Eugenie's School of the Dance.

The image of Diane and Cara when they were children, and the memory of their white-tighted missteps in their tutus, gave George a jab beneath his breastbone. He turned away from the crowd, and was about to soothe his soul with a cone from Friendly's when he heard the sound of coughing behind him, and turned back to see one of the contestants, a teenage girl, covering her mouth with fingers that ended in polka-dot painted nails.

"Could you do me a favor?" she asked him, when he made the mistake of meeting her eyes, which looked dark in the hollow of black shade powdered above the lids. "I just ran out of cigarettes. Would you buy me a pack?"

The girl was slim, and had hair the color of fresh tar floating up from her forehead in stiff spirals and stretching in the opposite direction toward the seat of her jeans, where THE GAP was stitched across the pocket. She stood straight against the vertical woodpiece of the money tree, her fingers pressed sturdily around a fistful of dollar bills, her feet in their faded sneakers planted flat on the plywood floor. She looked to George only a year or two older than Cara, although he supposed the plucky squint of this girl's eyes would fool many people into taking her for a grown-up.

But on closer inspection he saw that the bangs of her sweet black hair had been dyed maroon, and in the lobe of each ear she wore two turquoise studded posts, one with a silver beetle crawling downward to her neck. Her sweatshirt had been turned inside out, and the sleeves had been ripped open at the seam. These signs of conformism made him wince.

"You shouldn't be smoking," he said automatically. "You're too young."

"What are you, my father?" The sneer in her voice was so familiar he could not help loving it, though he knew this to be perverse. "Forget I asked, then. I thought you looked okay." She began searching the crowd.

"Wait," George said, almost without realizing it, "I'll do it." She might have picked someone she shouldn't have trusted, and he would never forgive himself. She smiled, as if she'd known she was going to win something. "I have some money in that bag down there," she told him, pointing with her free hand at her feet. George bent and lifted a blue duffel with a TAKING CARE OF BUSINESS button stuck inside the fabric. He held it open before her, smelling the perfume of violets, and averted his eyes as she rummaged through the things inside.

"Here," she said, scooping up a dollar and some change with one hand, straining to keep the other in the air and fastened around the cash. "Anything except mentholated. Menthol makes me puke." George took the money and put the bag back down by her feet. He threaded his way through the crowd and toward the cashier's counter at CVS.

When he came back with the lowest tar brand he could find, he saw that one of the male contestants, the collegiate-looking boy in a Mets cap, had given up. Letting his arm swing down from the air with a groan of relief, he swore softly and flicked with contempt at a dollar bill floating above his head. "We are down to four competitors, ladies and gentlemen," the announcer said, "and we're closing in on a full eight hours of *funds* and games." A collective cluck of amused disgust passed among the spectators.

"Oh, my God," the girl said, taking the pack of cigarettes from George. "That man should be shot." She ripped off the cellophane covering with her teeth and shook one out. Feeling like a criminal, George lit it for her. The murmur of other spectators buzzing around him, together with the idea of playing so curious a game of hooky on a Saturday afternoon, gave him the courage to keep talking. "Doesn't your arm get tired up there?" he asked, then more boldly, "What if you have to go to the bathroom?"

The girl brushed her long hair back over her shoulder, as if the motion helped her generate her answer. He was heartened by the fact that when she took smoke in, it came out again quickly. "They gave us a ten-minute break around noon," she said. "Everybody ran to the john, then pounded back some pizza, and came back to resume the touch at ten after. One guy missed the buzzer by two seconds, and they gave him the boot."

"That doesn't seem fair."

"Really." She wrapped her dark mouth around the cigarette and pulled thinly. "Oh, jeez," she said then, looking up beyond George and into the crowd. "Here we go."

A boy who looked about twelve had maneuvered his way through the throng to stand next to George. "Grace, you coming or not?" the boy said. He had the same black hair as the girl, but instead of hanging down his back it was cropped short, just under his ears, and had been cut so recently that George could make out the red scissor nicks in his neck. The boy's speech addressed the floor in a rigid mumble.

"Do I look like I'm about to go with you, Henry?" the girl said. "Do you think I've been hanging here with my arm straight up in the air for eight hours because I intend to lose this money?" From the way the girl spoke, George could tell she was the boy's sister. Henry shifted his weight from one leg to the other, and his red jacket hung askew from his shoulders, dripping remnants of rain.

"Please, Grace," he said. "It'll make him so happy."

"In that case you can *positively* forget it," Grace said. "Leave me alone here, Hen. You all go on. Tell him I am otherwise engaged at the moment. Tell him to go jump in the lake. Tell him—"

"*Okay*, Grace," the boy said. "I get the message." He stood looking at the packets of money hanging from the wooden bars, a rotating galaxy of cash. The other people whose hands were attached to the green piles blinked back at him without interest. "If you win, can I borrow enough for a couple of Pink Floyd tapes? I'll pay you back someday, I promise."

"We'll see, Henry," she said. "Now get out of here, okay? I'm getting sick of your face." The boy lingered a silent moment, then turned and made his way back toward the Sears exit.

"That was my brother," the girl said.

"So I gathered," George replied. Around them the crowd of spectators swelled and dwindled to the odd rhythm of window-shoppers, ice cream—eaters, and stroller-pushers clicking across the mall. He looked out at the soft blobs of face and wondered what they made of him up here, half-crouched on the platform beside the peculiar money contraption and the girl with the purple hair.

"They probably think I'm your father," he said to her.

"Oh, God forbid," she said, and then she saw what her answer had done to his face. "Wait, I didn't mean that the way it sounded. I was just thinking that *one* is more than I can handle right now. Fathers, I mean."

"Is yours a problem?" George prepared himself for confidences of physical and emotional mistreatment. He felt thrilled and nervous at the same time.

"Problem is not the *word*. Do you know why Henry was just in here trying to get me to give up this contest?"

"No. Why?"

"Because they're going to a stupid Yankees game tonight, and they want me to come with them. Can you imagine, on a day like this? Look at these people. They're all sopping like jerks."

George felt his toes squishing around inside his loafers. "It might not be raining down in the city," he pointed out. "Besides, there is a tarp."

"Well," said Grace, "that's not the *point*." She put her free hand up behind her neck and kneaded the muscles there. Next to her, the woman with the untucked blouse let out a sigh, and her hand dropped heavily from her designated cluster of bills.

"I've had it," she announced, and the umber-suited man rushed over with his megaphone.

"Ladies and gentlemen! We've got another loser!" The woman gave him a dirty look, tucked in her blouse, and stepped off the platform with a high-heeled clunk. "We're down to three contestants now, and it's been eight hours and sixteen minutes since we started. Let's have another round of applause for our finalists!" This time the clapping was louder, and George saw that the crowd had expanded on all sides, out to the toy store and beyond Baskin Robbins.

"You could actually do it," he said to Grace, excited by the thought that he might be standing next to the winner when it was all over. He tried to think how he would explain it to Ginny, if he made the news on TV.

"I *better* win," Grace said. "I have big plans for this money."

"Do you?" He wondered for a moment what his own daughters might do with a windfall of five hundred dollars. He would suggest that Cara put it aside for college in two years, he decided. Diane might offer to help pay for her new braces.

"Yeah," said Grace. "I'm going down to visit Elvis."

"Presley?" For an instant George was embarrassed, thinking he had dated himself irreparably, but Grace nodded.

"Yeah. You must know about it, right? How every year

they open up the Graceland mansion in Memphis, on the anniversary of the day he died? August sixteenth, it is. That's this coming Monday. People get to go in and see where he lived, and buy belts and stuff, and key chains with his face on them, and you can even buy a little bottle of his sweat, I heard. And then you can actually go and see his gravestone at the Meditation Gardens." Her voice vibrated with reverence. "There's a charter bus leaving from Schenectady tomorrow, and I'm going to be on it. And there's not a single thing my father can do to stop me."

"He doesn't want you to go," George guessed.

"Are you kidding? He had a meltdown when I told him." She reached up to adjust a tangled earring. "See, I'm basically broke, and when I asked him could I borrow a few bucks for this trip, he said no way am I going to give you my hard-earned money to worship some old greaser who isn't even alive anymore. If he was having a concert, Dad said, that's one thing. Dead, he's another story." She flipped her cigarette to the platform below her and ground the butt in with her sneaker heel.

"I said, but Dad, he was part of *your* whole generation, don't you want me to know more about history? And *he* said, don't give me that, I know you only want to go because that throwback boyfriend of yours put it into your head. And *I* said, well, Rex and I are going whether you like it or not, and he said, no, you're not, and I said, you just watch. So when I heard about this contest and the money you could win, I figured it had to be some kind of cosmic message, you know? I was the first one in line this morning outside the store. With five hundred dollars I can pay for my fare and Rex's, and I'll probably even have enough left over to buy an Elvis momentum for Henry." Delicately, she spit a piece of her own hair out of her mouth.

"Does your boyfriend play music?"

"Oh, my God. You should hear him." Grace spoke even faster as her eyes narrowed with pride. "Elvis is Rex's personal hero. He's home right now writing a song to bury somewhere near the mansion. It's called 'Elvis, We Owe

You One.' Rex talks just like him, and listen to this, Rex even means *king* in Latin or something. Not to *mention* my name, Grace, and Grace-*land*." She shook her head and smiled, as if the coincidence was barely within the scope of her belief. "We've seen *Blue Hawaii* together four times, and he knows all the songs by heart." George felt a vague volt of pleasure at this information. He had taken Ginny to see the same movie on one of their first dates.

"Grace?" He heard the thin voice behind him, and turning he saw Henry at his shoulder again, looking up and tapping the Touch-A-Thon platform with the toe of his sneaker.

"Hi," George said, feeling now like a friend of the family.

"Hello," Henry said. "Grace, Dad says if we don't leave in *ten* minutes, we're going to be late for the game."

"So, who's stopping you?" From her position under the high bar, Grace looked down on her brother with disdain. "I already *told* you, I'm not going. I'm staying here until I win this money, and then tomorrow Rex and I are heading down to Memphis. To visit *Elvis*."

"Grace, we've been waiting in the car for an hour and a half now. Mom says if she sees one more idiot parking job she's going to commit suicide. Dad's too stubborn to come in here, but you *know* how much he wants you to go with us."

"Then tell him he can stop making fun of my hair. And tell him it's none of his business how many times I get my ears pierced, they're my ears and I'll put twenty holes apiece in them if I feel like it."

"Do you get down to see the Yankees much?" George asked.

"No, we don't. That's the whole *point*." Henry spoke in his sister's pained italics. "We only go once a year, together, for the Old Timers Game. Dad used to be a batboy, and some of the guys still remember him when we go down there. Once Yogi Berra recognized him in the stands and let him come out on the field to sub for half an inning. Dad made us wait around afterward in case anybody wanted an autograph."

"I remember Yogi," George said. He thought of the way the bat sounded cracking the ball over radio static.

"After the game, we always go over to the house of this friend of Dad's, that used to batboy with him, who lives in Brooklyn, and we have this picnic and a softball game. It's the corniest thing going, but Dad loves it. He wears his old cap even though it doesn't fit anymore, it keeps sliding off his head. Anyway it's a *tradition*." Henry turned back to glare at his sister.

"If he wants me to come, Hen, he can march himself in here and beg me," Grace said in a slightly softer tone, then added, more loudly, "not that it would make a sweet bit of difference in the long run."

"But he won't give in this time," Henry protested, "not after that fight last night. You should never have called him that name."

"Forget it, Henry." Grace was turning her face away from him, toward the other side of the Touch-A-Thon platform. She held firm to the money inside her fingers. "You just go out and tell him to start driving already, and tell Mom to cool her jets. Go *on*," she told him, and Henry turned around with a sullen clucking noise and faded back through the crowd.

The woman with the bandanna wrapped around her curls, who stood at the packet of cash next to Grace, began to wail. "I can't stand it anymore," she said, and let her sweatered arm fall from her section of the wood bar. A muttering passed through the assembly as the two remaining competitors, Grace and the man with the perspiration stains running down his shirt, faced each other under the crosspiece.

"I'm going to win," she whispered down to George. "That guy won't be able to hold on much longer. He'll roll right off in his own fat lard."

"You may be right," George said. But he was picturing Henry and his parents out in the parking lot, Henry punching his fist crossly into a small mitt, his mother urging his father not to smoke in the closed car while they waited for Grace to come out.

"I bet they're still waiting," he said to her suddenly. "I bet you could catch them before they leave, if you changed your mind and decided to go with them."

"Are you kidding? Give up *now*?" But the excessive incredulity in her voice made him believe the idea had occurred to her as well. "No way," she said then firmly. "I've been standing here like this all day, and I am going to win this money, and I'm going to see where they planted Elvis when he kicked. And I'm sorry, but I'm just too old to be caring about some stupid baseball game that doesn't even count in the standings."

"Why don't you just wait until next year to see Elvis?" George asked her. "You said people make the trip to Memphis every anniversary. I've seen pictures in the paper. It's an annual event, like a pilgrimage or something."

Grace looked down at him, and then away from his face to the rest of the crowd. "Because next year I might not care." She raised her eyes again and spotted something beyond her. "Oh, God," she said, but this time George saw that the words were twisted around an involuntary smile. He looked out and recognized without having ever seen them before the shape of her parents standing to one side of the audience, watching their daughter on stage. Her father held a camera up to his eyes and sent a flash off, and her mother waved in spite of herself. Henry stood to one side, chewing gum with his mouth open.

"Ladies and gentlemen! We are down to the final two contenders in the first annual Lady Love Cash Touch-A-Thon!" The announcer swayed before the front of the wooden bars, drawing spectators in with a long wave of his arm. "How long can they last? Who will be our Touch-A-Thon crown winner?"

The fat man looked over at Grace and said, "You may as well pack it in right now, honey. They'll have to blast me offa here with a blow torch before I give up this cash."

"Me too," Grace told him, straightening, with a turn of her back from where her parents stood and a resolute readjustment of her grip on the money above her head.

"Well," George said. He felt spreading through him the familiar sensation of being stepped over. "I guess I'll be going, then." He waited, wanting her to object, to put an arm out and let her hair fall onto his sleeve; but she said nothing. From the corner of his eye he saw her parents making their way not forward but back to the main exit of the mall, Henry trudging behind them. He could feel Grace watching the hole they left in the stagnant crowd. "Can I tell you something?" he said, and she waited with a frown that reflected not confusion but the struggle of trying to decide.

"I think you're a good girl." He did not know where the words came from or what emboldened him to say them, but there were more. "And I hope Elvis is worth it." She kept watching him with that sharp fold of the forehead, those suspicious eyes, and he knew he had gone too far. "I'm sorry," he said, and thinking it was the best thing to do he turned away from the platform, and began to push downhearted through the hordes.

He took a few steps. There was a weighty silence, followed by the soft shuffle of sneaker on the wood behind him. "Hey," Grace called, and he stepped back toward the center, feeling chilled and hopeful.

She snatched up her duffel bag and jumped down from the platform, leaving cash swinging in her wake. Her drop pushed her forward and she fell into George, and in putting her arms out for balance she grabbed hold of his shirt and lingered against it a moment longer than he guessed she would have needed to steady herself. "All right I'm *going*, are you *happy* now?" she said as she pulled away, and he watched the long sheet of hair bob hurriedly through the crowd and out toward the parking lot.

"Ladies and gentlemen, the Touch-A-Thon is over!" George heard the announcement behind him as he separated himself from the applause and walked out to his own car, stopping along the way to buy two record albums, one of Elvis Presley and the other of Pink Floyd. On the car radio he heard that the rain had let up in New York City, and the Old Timers Game would be played as scheduled. Yogi Berra was going to be a captain.

When he got home, Ginny was chopping onions under the faucet. The laundry lay folded in neat piles on the table, and beneath it the dog was putting her paws over her eyes, as the rain beat down. Diane and Cara were painting their fingernails, Diane with a pale pink, Cara a bolder lilac. They looked up briefly as George stepped into the house and shook the water from his windbreaker.

"How was the movie?" he asked the girls.

"It was okay," Diane said. "Except we didn't have enough money for popcorn, Dad, you forgot to give us our allowance."

"You owe me *two*," Cara reported.

"Where've you been?" Ginny asked. "I thought you were going to get to the trash compactor today."

"I will," George said. "I went over to the new mall."

"Did you see Debbie Mastello?" Cara said. "At the Cake-n-Cookie? You couldn't miss her if she was working. The girl is pork on *wheels*."

"No," George said. "They were having this contest, the Touch-A-Thon it was called, to see who could keep their hands up in the air the longest, touching this money. They started out with twelve people this morning, but by the time I saw it there were only five left. I met one of the women in the contest. Her name was Grace. She asked me to buy her some cigarettes, and we got talking."

"Aha, a woman named Grace," Ginny said. She was smiling into the sink. "A likely story."

"So what *happened*?" Diane asked him. "In the *contest*?"

George sat down next to the girls and let them paint one of his fingernails with a mixture from their bottles. "Well," he told them. "I won."

**WELCOME
TO
OUR
VILLAGE**

WELCOME TO OUR VILLAGE

Kat woke up with cotton between her eyeballs and the taste of sand in her mouth, and someone had nailed her skull to the bedpost. "What's wrong with *you*," her sister Sheila said from across the room, where she was clipping purple squares out of construction paper. Kat stood up, not answering, and trembled past her sister to the bathroom. It had been a long, late night.

When she came out, clean and dripping from her shower, she felt better. "I didn't get much sleep, is all," she said to Sheila, patting her hair dry between sides of a towel. She moved closer to Sheila's desk, and bent over to see what her sister was doing.

"They're supposed to be place cards," Sheila said. She pointed to the names scripted carefully across each folded square in black felt marker: Mom, Dad, Sheila, Kat. Grandma, Richard, Miriam, and Hannah. Her voice carried something suspicious in it. "If you weren't so hungover, you might remember that I do this *every* Thanksgiving," Sheila said, not snottily, but with a sophistication that did not belong to her.

Kat paused in plucking her jeans from the dresser, and looked away from her sister because she was going to lie. "I wasn't drunk, sweetie," she said, watching bolts of sun lightning explode in front of her eyes. "I *love* those flowers," she added, pointing to the clumsy daisies bleeding from Sheila's pen. Her sister's disgusted look did not invite her to continue, so she padded out of the bedroom and down the stairs, misbuttoning her sweater.

"Bitch," Kat said, on her way down.

In the kitchen, her mother had put the turkey in the oven and was working on last night's crossword. "There's some juice in the fridge," she told Kat, pressing down on the eraser until some of the squares themselves were almost obliterated. Then she said, "We didn't hear you come in last night."

Kat sighed and poured a finger of orange juice into her favorite Buffalo Bills glass. She would dump it in the sink when her mother wasn't looking. "It wasn't all that late, Mom," she said. "Besides, I'm a big girl now, remember."

"Well," her mother said. "I guess that goes without saying, doesn't it?" If it hadn't been Thanksgiving she might have said more, but as it was she only shrugged her bathrobe up higher on her shoulders, and set her pencil on the page again.

"Four-letter word for a spotted rodent," she murmured, and that was the end of it.

Kat carried her glass into the living room and set it on the window ledge near the front door. Outside it was sunny, blue-skied, even summery, not gray and dismal like every other Thanksgiving she remembered. She hated the morning for its miserable brightness.

"What time are people coming?" she said, squinting hard at the sun.

"Noonish." Her mother paused in the middle of a coffee sip. "Can you think of a word for an Australian tambourine?"

Kat said, "No" and moved closer to the window. In the yard, she could see her father collecting frozen pine cones up from the lawn and putting them in a Macy's shopping bag. He was wearing his red-and-black flecked shirt, and he looked like a weird, nervous bird, bobbing in and out around the branches of the tree, stooping to pick up the cones and straightening up again with a darting, nimble swoop. He never knew what to do with the cones once he got them off the ground; he liked to have the yard cleared, but he could never bring himself to throw the cones away. Bags of them lined the garage walls in worthless symmetry. Now, stopping to arch his back, with his hand on his spine, her father caught sight of her standing in the window. He hesitated for a moment, then nodded to greet her gaze. Kat put her hands up to the cold glass and pressed hard. The moons of her fingertips turned bloodless as a baby's, and she thought she might fall through.

Her grandmother was the first to arrive, bearing pies made of pumpkin and mincemeat. "I don't know why I don't just use the canned filling like everybody else," she said, as Kat's mother lifted the wax paper covering to take an admiring whiff. "Cutting up that pumpkin and scooping out those strings. All that trouble—I don't think I can stand it another year." It was the same thing she said every Thanksgiving.

Sheila was in the dining room, arranging flowers for the middle of the table. Kat and her grandmother settled in the living room on opposite ends of the couch, and Kat's father came in and began to build a fire, tossing logs across the hearth in his careful, measured way. "Don't let that sun fool you," he said, to no one in particular. "It's cold out there." When he went to look for matches, Kat was unexpectedly left alone with her grandmother, and they looked at each other by mistake as both raised their eyes to the clock.

"Well," her grandmother said, as if this chance contact were a commitment to speak. "I know we're not supposed to talk about it around here, but that baby's got a birthday coming up, isn't that right?" She was working a needle up and down on a patch of cloth, and Kat saw she was filling in the design of a clown with buck teeth and a red flower-nose. A Christmas gift for Hannah, she supposed.

"Mmm," she said, meaning yes, although she had never thought of it exactly that way—as a birthday.

"I thought so," her grandmother said. She stopped sewing and looked over the top of her eyeglasses at Kat. "I never told you this, but all that time you were in the hospital,

I was praying that baby would survive. Even when they said it looked so bad, with the breathing problems, I prayed it wouldn't die and leave you with nothing to remember. I still don't believe a granddaughter of mine went out and got herself in trouble, and Lord knows I never hear the end of it at church, but nobody in this day and age deserves their baby to die." She leaned back over her pattern and mumbled, further, "And you only seventeen."

"Eighteen, now," Kat said, but her grandmother didn't hear her. Kat got up and went into the pantry, shut the door behind her, and poured vodka in her orange juice. She had no use for God, although she was intrigued by the calm that came into her grandmother's eyes when she talked about church and prayer. Her grandmother said it was a miracle the baby ended up living, in spite of what the doctors predicted, and at first Kat thought she might be right. But then it came to her that certain things just happened, and they had nothing to do with God. Maybe her baby was meant to grow up and become a president, or a scientist, or an opera singer; who could tell? Kat was not good at anticipating. She only wished she were as sure as her grandmother that it was a blessing the baby didn't die.

The baby was a girl. She had wanted to call her Katherine after herself, but the foster parents renamed her Jane, after the doctor who had finger-pressed the little blue chest to finally save her life. That much Kat had been able to find out from the file at the adoption agency, by reading upside-down when the woman at the desk wasn't watching. She looked it up in a Name-the-Baby book at the library: Jane meant "God's gracious gift." There it was again. She looked up Katherine. It meant *pure*. Well, that showed how much they knew.

The foster parents were going to adopt the baby and move to another city. Kat didn't know their name, and standing in the pantry she wondered for a minute about where her baby would grow up, until she remembered that it didn't matter to her. She stepped back into the kitchen, and her mother was looking at her with narrow eyes.

"I just hope that's plain orange juice you're drinking," she said. "Your father and I have been pretty forgiving lately and looked the other way, but if you get drunk today, you'll spoil things for everybody." She had changed from her robe into a skirt and sweater, and she smelled of Wind Song perfume. Her hair was pulled back in a barrette shaped like an ear of Indian corn.

"*Okay*, Mom," Kat said, taking another sip, and then so her mother couldn't hear she whispered "Jesus." She went back into the living room, and without consulting her grandmother she turned on the TV.

"Wait—this isn't the best parade," Sheila protested, coming into the room and reaching for the TV Guide. "The one on Channel Ten has Michael Jackson doing 'Beat It' on a float with the Muppets. I saw them practicing on 'Good Morning America.'"

"Don't you know anything?" Kat said. She was irritated because her drink was almost gone, and because her mother had caught her again. "Nobody really sings on those things. The stars are only mouthing the words, and somebody plays a tape behind the floats. You mean you never noticed how their lips don't move with the music?"

"Oh," Sheila said, after a moment. "Well, I don't care." But she let her hand fall from the channel dial, and went back into the dining room to fiddle with the centerpiece.

Her grandmother wrapped a piece of thread around her fingers, and pulled so tightly it snapped. "Do you always have to pull everyone else down with you?" she said to Kat, tying off a knot.

The night before, she had gone out with Duncan and Steve and Walt, to celebrate the Thanksgiving vacation. "Holidays are always the best excuse to get wasted," Duncan had said, opening a bottle of Bully Hilly and taking the first slug. "I mean, we can't ignore tradition." They were drinking in the back of Duncan's van because Kat was under age, and besides, bars were too expensive and too loud. They preferred their own company to anyone else's, anyway. All through high school they had gotten to know each other like family, all five of them—Craig was the only one missing now—and they were more comfortable than siblings. "I think the last time we did this was the night of graduation," Duncan added. They were all a year ahead of Kat, in jobs or college now, and they had not had a reunion since that celebration in summer.

Kat got the bottle last and, taking a wet swallow, closed her eyes as the wine went down warm and sour. She leaned back on the pillow she'd given Duncan two Christmases ago: it was an orange and purple rectangle, and on the corduroy cover she had embroidered, clumsily, THE FOOD-MOBILE RIDES AGAIN, because he always kept boxes of glazed doughnuts and Hershey's kisses under the front seat, for when they got the munchies. He'd said it was the best present he'd gotten, next to a pipe his sister had bought him at a dress shop in Provincetown. For Kat's present he'd given her Pat Benatar's *Crimes of Passion.*

None of them had ever asked her anything directly about the baby before, but as they sat there in the van, the windows black with night and *Running on Empty* playing over and over, the birth now more history than truth and the wine in their bodies like boldness inhaled, she felt their questions and knew Walt would be the one to voice them.

"You don't have to talk about it if you don't want to, Kat," he told her, and knowing what was coming she put her hand out for the bottle and somebody passed it to her. "But that couldn't be true, what my sister heard from Vicky Vernetti, was it? That your parents didn't know you were—*you* know—until it was almost born? I mean, my mother says she can tell when my sister's on the rag, just by looking at her."

"Well, I guess mine never looked," Kat said, and laughed loudly, as if she had made a joke. But she saw that they were serious, and to make them feel better she said, "Vicky Vernetti is a lying slut." She was surprised they had even asked the question, because she thought they knew her well enough to answer it for themselves. It was true. She had always been able to keep her own secrets.

"Craig knew all along," she told Walt. "That's why he went away. Has anybody heard from him?"

They all shook their heads, and Kat felt her hopes drop. "Me either," she said. "He probably has some new chick at school. He's probably forgotten all about us." But this sounded like someone else talking, so she shut up and settled back into the pillow. "There must be another bottle around here somewhere," she said, letting the empty one roll under the seat.

Later, she moved closer to Duncan and lay her head on his chest, and then put her face up to his, to kiss him. She had never let him or Walt or Steve do anything more, because that was just for Craig, but at those times when she needed to be close to someone she turned to one of the others; they understood her and it was good, they were together for a while and she felt something, instead of feeling nothing. And now she needed it and she was willing to give; it didn't matter that it was not Craig; what was there left to save? But Duncan pulled his face away, and reached down awkwardly to touch her hair instead.

"Kat," he said, quietly. "I don't—we can't. It's different, now." He smelled of the wine but his voice was sober, and lifting her head Kat saw in his eyes that it *was* different, and she could not imagine how stupid she had been, to think that it would ever be the same, that they could ever understand her. She sat up and they pulled away from each other, and she was alone again.

Duncan had moved to the front of the van to change the tape. He put on "Jane's Getting Serious," which was one of Kat's favorite songs, and she began to sing along with it, losing herself dizzily in the beat. Steve and Walt, who were sprawled across the carpet, woke up and finished the last of the third bottle. "Hey," Steve said, watching Kat move her head to the music. "Jane. Isn't that the little bastard's name? Or should I say bastard-ette?" He ducked as Duncan threw the Foodmobile pillow at him, then stuck the pillow under his elbow and leaned against his fist. "Sorry," he said to Kat, but Kat saw he was not sorry at all.

She got up suddenly, and their faces came rushing at her and then beyond her, to a place she couldn't see. "I named her Katherine," she said, and the name felt like cleanser in her soiled mouth. Then she told them, the words sounding foreign, "I want to go home now."

By the time Richard and Miriam came, carrying Hannah between them in a baby seat, Kat was well into her fourth screwdriver, and feeling much better. As they burst into the house with blankets and diaper bags and rattles spilling onto the floor, she went into the kitchen with the rest of the family to greet them, feeling almost happy.

"Look at this little *doll*," Kat's mother said in a baby voice, rubbing a finger across Hannah's cheek. She stuck her face out to kiss Richard, and put a hand on Miriam's shoulder as Miriam carried the baby to the kitchen counter and set down the seat. Richard and Miriam lived out in Arizona, and this was the first time any of them had seen Hannah, who was almost five months old. Everybody crowded around—like idiots, Kat thought, but she did not want to step away—to look at the little face in the pink snowsuit hood.

"She looks just like both of you," Kat's mother said, inaccurately but with pride. Kat saw Richard and Miriam look at each other and smile.

"Well, bring her in here and let her watch the parade," Kat's grandmother ordered, hiding her needlepoint clown behind the toaster oven. "Put her down there, and let's see what she can do."

"I bet she can't *do* much," Sheila whispered to Kat, as they followed their grandmother into the living room. "I bet all she ever *does* is spit up."

Kat was about to add something crude, but then she realized Sheila had forgiven her for their fight earlier, so all she did was nod and answer, "I bet you're right." They sat in front of the fire to shield the baby from the spitting sparks, and she finished her latest drink and set the glass down, and watched as Miriam undid all the pink clothing and pulled Hannah out and held her in her lap.

"She sleeps through the night now," Richard announced. He put his hand on Miriam's knee and leaned over to push his nose into Hannah's. Watching them, Kat thought about how awkward it had been when her brother had first started going out with Miriam, because she was Jewish, and because she was different in a way that had nothing to do with religion. She was feisty, forthright, and passionate; she was a hugger, coming into a family that never hugged, and she did not hesitate to yell when she was angry, or cry when she was hurt. It had been four years since Miriam had married Richard, and Kat still felt she did not know her sister-in-law, although she was jealous of the way Miriam had come to be known by the rest of the family, even her grandmother, who had sent Miriam for Hanukkah last year an embroidered six-point star.

"So what's the verdict?" Richard said to his parents, as they leaned forward on the couch to look down at the baby. Kat's father had gotten his camera out, and was sticking it in Hannah's face. Sheila was trying to make the baby laugh, by waggling her tongue in the air behind her father's head.

"Not bad for your first shot at a granddaughter, is she?" Richard said.

The camera came down suddenly and at the same time Miriam moved to put an elbow in Richard's side, but it was too late. Kat felt them all looking at her, but trying not to, and she felt her face flush as she stood up and almost fell on top of Hannah.

"Wait—I didn't *mean* anything," Richard said, as she stumbled out of the room. In the kitchen she put an arm out to steady herself against the wall, and heard Richard apologizing.

"We just don't talk about it," her father said, his voice a distant mumble.

Miriam came into the kitchen and watched as Kat poured straight vodka into the bottle's cap and drank it off. "Well, that's helpful," Miriam said. "I'm glad you've found a way to deal with all of this."

"Shut up," Kat told her. "Would you leave me alone?"

"Everybody leaves you alone," Miriam said. "That's exactly the problem." She picked up a wet cloth from the sink to sponge off the place on her sleeve where Hannah had dribbled. "Listen. Do you want to get out of here for a while? Come skating with Sheila and me?"

"Skating? Mean on the ice?"

Miriam smiled. "No, in a bowl of Cheerios. Of course I mean on the ice. Sheila wrote me a letter. She told me you guys used to go every Thanksgiving, when you were little. And we have plenty of time before dinner, because Hannah Banana has to have her nap." Miriam moved cautiously toward Kat and took the bottle out of her hand. "Come on. It'll work up your appetite."

"Okay," Kat said, because it took too much energy not to.

She made her way up to the attic to look for her skates. The air was close and hot, and her tongue felt thick. She cleared away dolls, rumpled curtains, and stacks of *Ranger Rick* magazines from the top of the toy chest, then lifted the cedar lid. Her eyes began to water, and she swore at the dust she had stirred.

She reached for the skates and her hand brushed the white fur of a child's winter hat. She took the hat out slowly, rubbing her finger against its soft grain. Two pieces of yarn hung from the earflaps, ending in soft white balls. Kat tied the yarn in a bow, causing the balls to nestle together, and she held them up under her chin, the smell of the warm wool making her stomach roll.

When she was eight, all the Sunday School classes had been grouped together to put on a play about a boy who traveled around the world in a balloon. One of the places he landed was in an arctic village. Because her mother had just bought her the hat, Kat persuaded the Sunday School teacher to let her take the part of an Eskimo, even though everyone else her age was only a bobsled dog.

They were all jealous, not because of the hat, which was queer, but because she had known how to use it to get something they all wanted. Kat had been given the opening line in the scene; waving her mittened hand toward the other Eskimos, she was supposed to greet the traveler with a loud and friendly, "Welcome to our village!"

But when she got onstage, the hat made sweat drip in her eyes, and the harder she rubbed them, the more they stung. Then she began to feel sick inside her snowsuit. Moving a glacier in front of her so no one could see, she took off one of her boots and vomited into it. When she heard her cue coming up, she put her boot back on and stood up. "Welcome to our village," she whispered just in time, still tasting sickness in her throat, her voice shaking and her heart off its beat.

Afterward her father went out of the church to light a cigarette while her mother came back to the coat room to pick her up. "You didn't say it loud enough," her mother leaned over to tell her. Kat had already cleaned up her soiled boot and tucked it into her bookbag so her mother wouldn't get mad. "We couldn't hear you out there."

Now Kat tossed the white hat over her shoulder, toward the windowsill littered with dead flies, and pulled out her skates by their blade guards. "Be careful," her mother called after them, when they had put Hannah to sleep and set off toward the pond. As she walked behind Sheila and Miriam, it occurred to Kat that in the whole of her lifetime, she must have heard her mother say the same thing a thousand times before.

The pond was down the street and around the corner from the house. On the way, Kat stayed behind Sheila and Miriam, trying to concentrate on the white ice slicks under her feet, hoping that if she fell she would have the sensibility enough to put her hands out to break it. She knew she was drunk. The cold air crackling in her nostrils helped a little, but when it came right down to it she could feel her head swaying as she walked, and every once in a while Miriam turned to look over her shoulder to make sure she was behaving, as if Kat were a puppy unleashed in a new neighborhood.

Usually there were dozens of kids stumbling around on the pond's smooth circle, but today the only people stringing on their skates when the three of them arrived were Patty Coogan, who was six, and her little sister Joyce. Joyce was struggling to put on her double-runners, and Patty was singing to her from the aerobics videotape Kat and everyone else on the block knew almost by heart, from hearing Mrs. Coogan's daily exercise routine through the sun-porch screen in the summer.

"Kick those legs up, watch that gut! Pelvic tilt means flatter butt!" Patty was chanting, as she swiveled her hips back and forth, holding one skated toe in the ice as a pivot. Following Sheila and Miriam to the bench next to the kids, Kat saw Miriam smiling at Patty's wiggles and her seductive, husky-sweet voice.

"When I was that age, the sexiest we got was 'I'm a Little Teapot,' " Miriam said.

Kat sat down and managed to get her skates on, surprised but grateful that her toes weren't cold even when she set her sock feet briefly on the ice to unknot the thick laces. She pulled them tight at the top, over her ankles, and stood up at the edge of the ice. Sheila and Miriam had already pushed off and were making a slow circle, huddling close and occasionally grabbing at each other's arms to keep from falling. Kat skated over behind them and listened to what they were saying.

"Are my ankles bending in?" she heard Miriam ask Sheila.

"No. And anyway, so are mine."

"You guys are doing great," Kat called ahead to them, feeling suddenly generous and lighthearted. She had not been skating in years, and had forgotten what it felt like to be on the ice, gliding, moving so easily so fast and not even having to think about how it was happening. Her head was still congested with the effects of the vodka, but the air moving against her face, and the little chips of ice that came up and landed in her hair, made her feel energetic and invincible. She fell in beside them and heard blades clicking on the ice behind her.

"Keep your *thighs* on the *prize*," Patty Coogan shouted, pulling her sister along by the mitten thumbs and sticking out her fanny.

"She's cute," Miriam said. "A little flirt though, I bet."

"All anybody ever talks about anymore is sex, sex, *sex*," Sheila said abruptly, slowing down and turning awkwardly to face them. "I can't believe it. Yesterday Audrey Forman said her mother was getting her the Pill, and last week, I heard, this girl in *fifth* grade left to have a baby."

"God," Miriam said.

"Do we have to talk about this?" Kat felt a swing of nausea, and put a mittened palm on her stomach to quell it.

"Why not?" Miriam asked.

"I want to," Sheila said.

"Well, I don't." Kat speeded up to pull ahead of them, digging her skates hard into the ice. Coming to a corner of the pond, she let one foot lead the other and tried to turn into a backward loop, but her blades caught on something and she fell, landing in the wet snowbank at the ice's edge. Sheila and Miriam came over and helped to pull her up.

"That's what you get for drinking," Sheila said.

Miriam brushed off the back of Kat's jacket. "Richard told me you used to be good," she said.

"What?"

"A good skater. Richard says you used to be the one everybody watched, to learn how to do it."

"I *am* good." Kat shrugged out of Miriam's hold and almost fell again, but managed to stay up, although she could feel herself tottering. "Watch this, if you don't believe me." She was annoyed by Miriam's doubts and Sheila's accusations, and spinning away from them she wanted to put as much distance behind her as she could. She took it easily down the stretch of the pond's length, then did a slow but accurate turn at the other end and began to move toward them again, picking up her speed. Ahead of her she could see them standing together clumsily, their arms hooked for support.

"Just stay right there," Kat yelled, nearing the middle of the pond. "Nobody move, and I'll stop right in front of you." She remembered how, as a kid, she used to play this game with Sheila, skating up to where her sister stood and at the last minute shifting her weight so that her skates turned to the side, halting her in a scrape of flying ice flakes. No one had ever done it as well as she did, approaching so fast and stopping so suddenly, so close. Sheila didn't even flinch as Kat neared her, she trusted it that much. Kat picked up her pace, coming over to where the two of them were standing.

"Wait!" Sheila cried, and Kat realized, too late and with a sickening rise in her throat, that she was out of control. She tried to stop, but then she was pitching forward into the ice, into her sister, and her blades were tearing at soft red flesh.

Sheila's screams seemed to be coming from Kat herself. She felt their ache hard in her chest. Then she prayed to pass out in the cold silence of snow, but something even colder, inside, kept her awake and shuddering.

At the hospital, Kat sat with Miriam and her mother as they waited for the doctor to come out of the examining room. Her mother turned her head away when Kat offered her a cup of coffee from the machine. "It's not enough to make yourself miserable, is it?" she said, keeping her voice low so no one else could hear. "You have to put the rest of us through it, too."

Kat drank the coffee herself. They were close enough that they could hear Sheila whimpering in the next room, and when she heard her sister shriek once in pain, with a short but violent outburst, Kat left her mother on the lounge couch, went into the ladies' room, and threw up. Then, still gripping the edges of the toilet bowl, she began to cry. It was an act she had imagined many times during the past year, but she had always held back at the last minute as if, once started, she would never be able to stop. But now it came easily, with a comfort she had not anticipated. When she felt strong enough she stood up and stepped out of the stall to rinse her face, then bent over to let fresh, quieter tears fall into the sink. She was no longer drunk, but it was too late now to matter.

After a while Miriam came in and found her leaning against the wall. "Are you all right?" she said.

"Me?" Kat looked at her with surprise. "I'm not the one who got the skate in the eye. I'm not the one you should be asking." She looked in the mirror and saw a swollen, flush-red face. It was just the way she had looked when she had the baby, spent with effort in the aftermath of panic. Then she had not recognized herself in the glass above the delivery room, but now the shaken, guilty face was becoming a familiar one, and she hated it.

"I'm just bad," she said to Miriam. "I always have been."

"Are you sure?" Miriam's face was serious, but her voice was amused, as if Kat had announced she wanted to become a nun.

"Yeah," Kat said. The word echoed against the sterile walls. "Ask anyone who knows me."

When they got home, Kat's father and Richard had arranged a place for Sheila on the couch in the living room, with pillows propped up and the blanket from her bed above the cushions. She had a thick white bandage over her eye, and her face was puffy where they had taken stitches, but the doctor had told them she would be back to normal in a few weeks, with only a trace of a scar. Her eyesight had been saved completely. Kat tried to apologize to her sister as they walked out to the car from the hospital, but Sheila waved away her efforts and even managed to smile with the undamaged side of her face.

"It was an accident," she told Kat firmly.

Their grandmother had kept the food going, and was rustling around the kitchen talking to herself. She fixed a plate for Sheila before the others sat down, but Sheila said she didn't want any. Instead, she asked Miriam if she could hold Hannah during the dinner.

"That way I won't be the only outcast," she said, and Miriam brought her the baby, fresh from her nap and bundled in a dry pink sleepsuit.

"I have to get a shot of this," Richard said, anxious to restore the holiday. He picked up their father's camera and aimed it at Sheila's bruises. "We'll put it in the photo album, under 'Family Tragedies.'"

"You mean with the ones from our wedding?" Miriam asked him, hitting him with a pink sleeve. The shutter clicked, and Hannah reached out her fat arms toward her father in a query of joy.

In the dining room, Kat's mother was pouring wine. "Don't think you're going to get any of this," she said to Kat, who had come up close behind her.

"I know," Kat said. "Don't you think I know?"

"Well," her mother answered, replacing the cork. "Good, I guess."

"Are we ready?" Kat's grandmother was pouring gravy into a bowl. "I need some help with this food, so get yourselves out here." They went into the kitchen and picked up dishes and trays, and carried them to the table. "Be careful of that cranberry sauce, it's sliding," her grandmother instructed. "Watch the stuffing, it's spilling over the sides." But finally all the food had been transported, and they set about finding the place cards Sheila had arranged earlier in the morning.

"Hey, nice job on the names," Miriam called to Sheila, when they were all seated.

"I know," Sheila called back. "Thanks." Kat could see her sister through the living-room doorway, making Hannah's hands do patty-cake. The light from the window bounced off Sheila's bandage and made it a part of her face, as if the eye itself had swelled in size and power.

Her grandmother put her hands together. "Well, who's

going to say the blessing?" she demanded. It was usually Sheila's job.

Kat looked up. Her mother was lifting lint from the table-cloth. Her father stood in his place behind the turkey, staring vacantly down at the platter, the carving knife poised at the leg joint in stagnant fingers. Richard and Miriam touched hands, and on the other side of the table Kat felt the quick tremble of memory at what this had been like; what it had been to reach for somebody and know he would reach back; what it had meant to be held for once and not let go too early.

"Let me," she rushed to offer, and as the faces of her family bent over their meal and a baby sang in the silence, she tried to remember a grace from her childhood.

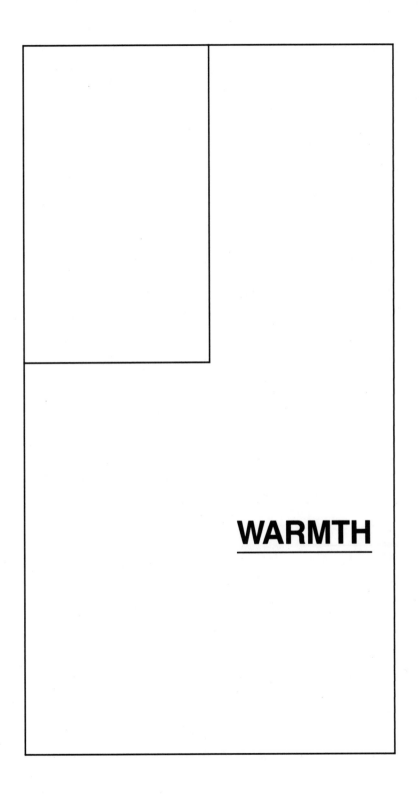

WARMTH

WARMTH

Gail was telling the rest of them about the mass murder that was the subject of her moot court case when the light over the table dimmed brown, bloomed back to bright yellow for an instant, then went out altogether above their heads.

"The thing was, he told his shrink he was going to kill these people, and then went out and did it," Gail had just finished saying. "It's a question of failure to warn, that's the legal term. They were forseeable victims." The last was spoken as the room went dark, and her words sounded hushed because no one could see her saying them. It was breakfast time, a Sunday, and outside the year's first snowstorm was falling, a freak in the beginning of October, loading the trees with a confusion of season, the double weight of red leaves and snow.

"Hey. What happened to the lights?" their mother said, getting up to flick the switch and turn on the radio. There was a burst of static, and it went dead.

"Wait a minute. I'll check the TV." Lindy, the youngest, could be heard punching and pulling buttons in the next room. "Uh oh," she said, coming back to the table. "This stinks."

"Oh, no. What are we going to do if the heat goes off? And everything in the freezer will spoil." They could see their mother's eyes worrying behind her glasses. Her voice always went low to a single note when she was upset, and it scared them, though they were all technically adults now and could technically take care of themselves.

"Come on, you guys, don't panic." Valerie, the oldest, lifted the funnies from the newspaper up against the gray morning light sliding in through the windowshade. She was one of those people who believe that if you merely refuse to acknowledge the unpleasant things happening around you, they will stop happening, or at least they will cease to be unpleasant. "It'll come back on in a minute. It's probably just a loose wire."

"Does this mean the curling iron won't work?" Lindy asked. "And the hair dryer too?"

"I'm more worried about you guys getting back safely," their mother said, her distraction continuing. She stood at the kitchen window, pulling the curtain back, watching the flakes fall and settle on branches, windshields, driveways, and garbage pails. "I hate to imagine you all driving in this. I don't think I should let you go."

"Mom, I have to get back today," Gail said, "whether you *let* me or not. Moot court's in the morning, and it's the biggest part of my grade."

"I need to leave, too," Valerie said, lowering the newspaper and for the first time allowing concern to enter her eyes as she looked out at the yard, where the picnic table sat buried beneath the wet white. Only two nights ago, Friday, they had sat around it celebrating their mother's birthday with hamburgers and champagne. "Bob needs the car tomorrow for a meeting in Providence."

"And I promised somebody I'd work for them tonight at the caf." Lindy waited to speak until her sisters had finished, the way they had trained her, over the years, without even knowing it. When she did get the words out, they came with spaces between, as if to make it easier for anyone who might decide to interrupt. She went over to join the others by the window, where they stood watching the snow, wondering.

"It's not *supposed* to snow in October," Gail said. She sounded annoyed.

"I am getting cold," Valerie admitted after a while.

Their mother, who was standing in front, turned to take them all into a hug. "What if we got trapped here forever?" she asked, and they tried not to notice the wishfulness in her smile. "What if no one could ever leave?"

By two o'clock they had gotten six inches—they knew because Lindy took a ruler outside and stuck it in the snow by the fencepost. Valerie brought in the portable radio from her car, and they tuned in to the station they had grown up waking to, their parents' standard, before they found out through their own sources about FM. There was no music today, only talk about the storm, which was the earliest and worst to hit the county in twenty years. They heard cancellations and closings and warnings about the slick roads.

"I have to go soon, I have to go," Gail said at intervals that grew closer together, looking up from her textbook, where every line on the page had been wrinkled by yellow highlighter. "Mom, I can't keep waiting for it to let up. If I leave now, I can probably get clear of it in an hour—they say it's not so bad heading south." She had the farthest to travel, and her expression was grim.

"Well," their mother said, tucking her socked feet under a sofa cushion. They had built a fire and each was huddled under a quilt, reading by windowlight, exchanging silent glances every time the man on the radio gave a new depth for the fallen snow. "I don't think it's a good idea, but I guess I can't stop you, if you've made up your mind."

"Hm." Gail had expected the opposition to be vehement. The rest of them sat and half-watched as she moved about the house packing her things up, shuffling with her bedspread wrapped around her shoulders, her hands snug in gardening gloves. She went outside to start her car, scrape and brush off the snow, slam the trunk down on top of her books and bags. Then she came back in and stood dripping snow on the carpet, waiting.

"Be careful, sweetheart," Valerie told her, kissing Gail's hair at the side of her ear. It was Gail and Lindy's joke that they were always deafened by their older sister's good-byes, which were dramatic and fearful, like wartime farewells. "Call us as soon as you get there, okay?"

"Who's the mother here?" their mother said, but she added, "She's right, honey—we want to know when you make it."

"Bye, Gail," Lindy said simply, giving a sweep wave across the distance between them. They stood at the door and watched as Gail backed the car out slowly, lights on, wiper blades clacking, tires spinning but allowing her to move. They waved at the old Chevette receding slowly up the street. Her departure changed the mood in the living room as the others returned to their places; now they could feel among them the silent presence of a prayer. Snow stuck to the windows in clumps, rising like wet silver up the panes. The man on the radio warned against driving.

"Shit," the girls' mother said.

Valerie looked up from the Sunday crossword and laughed. "I just realized why I have this headache. I haven't had coffee yet," she said. "You keep instant, don't you?"

"But the stove won't work," her mother reminded her.

"Well, I'll heat it up on the fire." Valerie went into the kitchen, trailing the afghan her grandmother had knitted when Valerie was a baby. It had evolved down through the sisters into a new pattern, with the unraveling and reknotting of flimsy yarns. She came back with a panful of water, crouched in front of the fireplace, and held it above the flames.

"This is just like 'Little House on the Prairie,' " Lindy said.

The sudden trill of the telephone made them all shiver. "Get that, will you, Half-Pint?" Valerie asked, snickering into her knee.

"Oh, hi," Lindy said into the receiver, after listening for a moment. "Well, I don't know. I'm not sure how much is out there. Just a sec." She covered the mouthpiece with her hand. "Dad wants to know if he can come over and borrow some wood for their fire. They're about to run out."

Their mother pushed a puff of air between her lips. It was

a familiar sound around the subject of their father. "If he wants to risk his life driving over here, that's fine with me," she said. She looked down at the page and then up again in the same motion. "Tell him he can bring back my punch bowl, while he's at it."

Lindy repeated this information, said "Okay," and hung up. "He's coming over," she reported. She stretched her long legs out on the rug and began lowering her nose to her knees.

"That always looks so painful," her mother said.

"It was, at first. But now my muscles are used to it." The sounds of her stretching and lifting, flexing and exhaling, filled the next half hour. Then she got up and lifted the heels of her sneakers one at a time behind her shoulder-blades. At the end of the routine she said, "Hey, Dad's here," and let her foot fall abruptly, hitting the piano bench with a thunk.

They stood at the kitchen door to watch. Their father parked near the end of the driveway and began to hunch his way toward them, his shoulders meeting the flakes first. He hugged the punch bowl close to his jacket, and made a mincing shuffle in the snow. "Oh, my God, he looks like an old lady," Lindy said, laughing. "Like he's on high heels or something." They opened the back door and urged him onward, like spectators cheering a racer toward the finish. When he got inside he shook his head, and ice slivers scattered over them all, and collected in the bottom of the glass bowl between his arms.

"Hi, guys," he said, kissing Valerie and Lindy, his wet skin leaving their cheeks cold. "Hi, babe," he said to their mother. "Happy belated birthday, by the way. The big five-one: Holy Jeez. You don't look a day over fifty, if you ask me."

She took the punch bowl and set it down in the sink. "Thanks." There was a pause, during which the girls held their breath. "How was that party?" was all she said, and they let the breath out.

"Oh, good, good," he answered, rubbing an ice chip into

the rug with his boot. "The usual phonies. But she got a couple of sales out of it, so I guess it was the right thing."

"Hm." The girls' mother opened the tap to let water fill the bowl. While they watched, she turned it over to empty it, then dried it completely, poking the design crevices in the glass with a toweled finger. When she was finished, she held it up to the windowlight, as if examining hidden damage only she knew to look for. Then she put it away.

"Go ahead and take some wood," she said. "We just got a cord delivered last week, so there should be plenty." They waited with him at the door while he blew on his hands and squinted at the white wind on the other side, gathering his nerve.

"How *is* Maura?" Lindy said, when he didn't move after a minute. Her mother and Valerie looked at each other; again her father looked down.

"Oh, great, great," he said quickly. "She's okay." He coughed a little. "She said maybe you girls might want to come over and see our place sometime. No big deal, just for coffee or somthing."

"No thanks," Valerie said.

"Maybe someday, later, okay?" Lindy took a step backward, knowing before she felt it that Valerie's arm would be closing in protection or warning around her shoulder. Their father shuddered and pulled his gloves finger by finger over his red hands, and moved to go outside, backing into the wind.

"Let's be careful out there!" Lindy shouted after him, but her mother had the door shut before she could finish the sentence. They watched him plod toward the back edge of the yard and the shed they shared with two neighbor families, which held a communal supply of firewood, lawnmowers, bicycles, ladders, and tools. The shed was set back from the power line behind the houses, and they lost sight of him a few yards beyond their own door. They had just started to settle into their blankets again when they heard a car's sharp toot coming near.

"Gail's back," Lindy said, looking, and they rose in a rush to meet her, too, at the door.

"The Thruway's closed," she told them, as she began to shed layers. "Everything's closed. They can't blame me if the roads are closed, can they? Act of God, that's the legal term." She sniffled hugely. "Is that Dad's car out there?"

"He came to pick up some wood. He's on his way to the shed."

"What is he, crazy? You let him go?" She stopped with her boot lifted halfway from the floor. Her voice had switched back to high gear.

"What's the matter?" Lindy said.

"There's all kinds of wires down. Didn't you hear on the radio? They keep telling people not to go outside, especially near trees. Two people got electrocuted so far, touching live wires in their backyards."

"Shit," the girls' mother said.

"Somebody should go get him." Lindy picked up the boots Gail had just pulled off, and shoved her feet so hard into them that they could hear the squish at the bottoms. She wound a scarf around her face like a mummy's mask.

"Lindy, don't be ridiculous. You can't go out there." Valerie took one end of the scarf and began to unwrap her sister.

"Get your hands off of me!"

Valerie's arms jerked in the air as if Lindy's voice had first punched and then thrust them away. "Don't use that tone of voice with me, you witch," she said, but she sounded as if she might cry.

They both waited for their mother to intervene the way she had when they were younger, ending the argument with a sharp protest or a command. But lately she only listened when two or the three of them quarreled, as if she happened to be overhearing strangers in a checkout line. "Aren't you going to say something?" Valerie asked her, begging with her eyes. But her mother only shrugged.

"You're old enough to work it out for yourselves." This took the fun out of fighting, and the girls felt ashamed.

"Look," Gail suggested, "let's all go out, and just watch where we're stepping. You guys could use the exercise."

"Thanks a lot," Valerie said.

"No, she's right." Their mother began to pull on her own boots, the duck ones they'd given her for Christmas last year along with magenta-patterned tights. Funky Mama, they called her when she wore the gifts together, and the nickname was so old by now that nobody bothered saying it this time. "I think we all need some fresh air. But let's hurry, before your father gets zapped."

"*Mom.*" Lindy's face was a mixture of amusement and alarm. But she followed the rest of them out into the snow, all of them lined up at the doorway, taking deep breaths, like people about to dive into dark water.

The snow was thick as it fell against their faces, and made breathing difficult. A few steps out, they could sense their toes and fingers numbing inside wool, and lifted their feet higher to keep the extremities warm. They stepped in the prints their father had made, taking giant strides and sinking in snow to their knees.

"I can almost see the sun," Lindy shouted, pointing, and at that moment a gust carried her cap across the yard.

"Don't be ridiculous," Valerie called back. She added, "My nose hairs are frozen."

"Thank you for sharing that with us," Gail said.

The trudged toward the shed, arms locked now, their necks wet and their foreheads dripping. "Look! There he is," Lindy said, but they had all already seen him, crouched forward close to the ground by the power line, his earflaps nudging the snow. "Dad!" she shrieked as she neared him, and the others felt their hearts skitter and pick up speed when they tried to hurry through drifts to the place where their father lay.

"Charlie? Oh, my God, Charlie, are you all right?" Behind them the girls felt their mother's body pushing them out of her way, cutting through snow quicker than any plow blade, reaching him first. Her words flew back at them in the wind, hitting their ears like ice pellets. "Charlie, did you touch something?" She moved forward to clutch his coat.

He lifted his face to her; the skin over his cheekbones was red and raw. The girls caught up and halted short in a circle around his hunched figure. He smiled, and began to struggle to his feet, his arm pulled toward the ground by a load of wood too heavy for him to handle. "What's the big deal?" he asked them. He seemed chagrined. "I just lost my balance, fell down on my ass." He had grasped the arm offered to him in straightening, but did not let it go even after he stood steady. The girls bent to take logs from the pile he had dropped in the snow, all of them watching but trying not to show it as their parents held onto each other and turned back toward the house.

"Dad, we thought you got electrocuted," Lindy yelled forward. "On a live wire."

He looked confused for a moment, then smiled again. "You mean you were worried about me, Barb?" he said, dipping his head toward her down-packed shoulder. She slapped at the head, not meaning anything, and in the end let it stay.

"They're not supposed to be doing stuff like that," Lindy whispered to her sisters. "He's supposed to love somebody else."

"Will you shut up for once?" But Valerie's voice wasn't mean, and Lindy did not feel offended. They pushed on behind their parents, swinging logs between them in the depths of an old bedsheet they found in the shed. It was faster getting back to the house than it had been leaving it, and at the door they congratulated each other on the hardiness of their adventure, and the haul they had made. In the kitchen the girls' mother filled the teakettle even before she had kicked off her boots, and went into the living room to hold it close to the fire. The girls went upstairs to the cold bedrooms to put on dry clothes, and their father spread his scarf out across the hearth. When they came back down, he was dialing the phone.

"I'm going to wait for the roads to clear up," he said into

it, turning his face to the wall as he spoke. The girls spread out quickly around the room, listening with their heads bent over their books. It was getting dark outside, and when their mother pulled the windowshade all the way up, they could see snow falling in sheets off the roof. "No, I don't think it would be better to take a chance. I'd get stranded somewhere. Why don't you go over to the Harveys' until I get back? They have a wood stove." He listened for a few seconds, and then murmured, "No. Can't you see how dangerous it is out there? I'll be home when I can." He let his voice drop even lower on the word *home*. Valerie and Gail looked at each other through the motion of Lindy's legs, which were pedaling an imaginary bicycle in the air; then they looked at their father. "Mind if I hang with you guys for a while?" he said.

"Yeah, *stay*," Lindy told him, letting her legs drop, and her sisters thanked her silently, with a look.

Their mother was poking the fire. Lindy and Gail made room for their father on the couch, and Valerie joined her mother in the loveseat. They passed the afternoon this way, shuffling through magazines, hugging pillows, sometimes getting up to add a log to the fire or take a handful of crackers from the box in the middle of the floor. They ate a can of spaghettios and one of tuna, and the end of the raisin bread. They played Trivial Pursuit until Gail began to lose and knocked the question cards over as she got up to go to the bathroom. They listened to the batteries in the radio die. Then, suddenly, it was night.

"So how do we keep from freezing to death while we sleep?" their father said, stretching his feet out, rotating them in circles through the air, where his toe joints cracked. There was no question that he would stay. A foot had fallen since the day's beginning, and the snow's crust was glazed over with frozen rain.

On the other side of the room, their mother drew her blanket more tightly around herself. "You take a warm body to bed with you," she told him. "Remember? It doesn't matter whose." She had meant to be funny but it came off in a tone that horrified her, and the worst of it was that she had heard the tone before. Her daughters looked at each other. There was no making it better, and no taking it back. "I guess we should all stay in here, by the fire," she hurried on, bending over to toss magazines out of the way.

"But the house will go up," the girls' father said.

"Don't be ridiculous, Charlie. It will not."

"Well, don't blame me if we all burn to death in our sleep."

"Whose house *is* it?" their mother said, lowering herself into her loveseat bed, shivering until the movement made her feel warm. The girls lay in their birth order from left to right, and Gail got the best of the arrangement, with heat on both sides from her sisters, and none of the draft they both felt at their backs. At the other end of the room, their father stretched out on the couch, and they could see he picked the most uncomfortable position to lie in, so that he would be awake some of the night to guard against sparks. Outside they could hear the top layer of snow being whipped across yards, beyond roofs, above treetops, and into space.

"Remember the Christmas Aunt Stell called while we were opening presents, and you said you loved what she sent you, Mom, and you told her you were trying it on, and she said, 'But why would you want to try on a hammock?' " Valerie started giggling before she could finish the story, but the rest of them already knew the punchline, so it didn't matter. Their father's laugh lingered under the covers, staccato and rumbling deep.

"Remember the time she sent those weird cheeses?" he asked. "I was in the bathroom for a week."

"I don't remember that," Valerie said.

Lindy told him, "Neither do I."

"Oh." They could almost hear him slapping his own forehead for stupidity. "I guess that was just last year." There was a pause as they all blinked in the darkness. Valerie got up to get a tissue, and Gail asked for one, too.

They blew their noses in unison. The shock of noise in

the silence made everyone wince. "Thank you for sharing that with us," Lindy said.

Lindy was the first of the children to awaken in the middle of the night. She knew what time it was, even though the clock wasn't working, because she often awoke at the same cluster of moments in her bed at school, and lying in the hard space between the wall and her desk, she stared at the ceiling where her roommate had hung a small bear by a noose as a joke, and listening to the roommate breathe she prayed for sleep again. It was half past three. Next to her, Gail was making noises through her nose. Lindy reached up to shake her shoulder. "Listen," she said, and then Valerie woke too.

Their eyes adjusted quickly, and they saw that their parents' couches were empty, their blankets gone, the cushions where their heads had rested lying skewed on upholstered arms. Sound dawned more gradually, seeking focus in the dark.

"Do you think she's in pain, or is that just—just—" But Gail's articulateness failed her, and she ended with a groan into the flesh of her arm, lying outstretched in the long wake of Valerie's hair.

"God. This is *so* embarrassing." Valerie pulled her quilt up and covered her head with it. Underneath, she could almost hear the hearts of her sisters keeping time with her own. "Get under here, you guys. Try to ignore it. Recite the alphabet backwards. Who knows all fifty states?"

"Should they be doing this?" Lindy's whisper held a tinge of hysteria. "I mean, since he's married to somebody else?"

"Legally, it's adultery," Gail told her. After a pause she added, "At least I think."

"Maybe this means something." Lindy sounded the way she did when she entered a sweepstakes. She expected to win every one. "Maybe they're changing their minds."

"Their *minds* have nothing to do with it," Valerie told her, and then she flinched as Gail gave her a fake slap with a mittened hand. The three of them huddled even closer as a rush of cold air swept under the door.

"You think this is the first time?" Lindy asked.

In the morning, the shine of sun on snow struck the angle of their mother's eyes. Turning out of the loveseat toward the floor where her daughters lay, she recognized a change in her blood, and moving to the radiator she placed a hand on it, knowing before she touched it what she would feel, and she swore, quietly, almost without voice, and when she switched the lamp on she closed her eyes against the light it gave her, and felt betrayed and already lonely, already alone.

The girls did not wake up beneath their covers. Across the room, the bigger couch was empty, the two pillows and comforter piled neatly at its end. When the phone rang, she went slowly to answer it, knowing who it was for, and why. With the intrusion of the ring she heard her daughters begin to move on the floor behind her. The sounds of their shifting made her heart clutch, as if something were being removed before anesthesia took hold. She picked up the receiver with a gasp she didn't know was coming and that no one else would hear.

Outside, he stood in hard snow, scraping the windshield, picking sharp chunks from under the wiper blades. The storm was over. It left a coat of ice so thick against glass that when he hauled off and whacked it as hard as he could, as if he were stabbing something, all that flew off were tiny shards. It was impossible to cut through. He paused a moment, wanting to cry, and turned his face to the sun.

"God," he said.

The back door of the house opened, and he heard his name. He looked, knowing whose the voice was, but as he moved toward it he was blinded, by bright snow and ice hanging from the roof and fluorescence from the kitchen absorbing the flesh of her face and fingers. He paused again, peering ahead into the brilliance, trying to see where her body ended and the reflection began.

**SOMETHING
FALLS**

to Deborah

SOMETHING
FALLS

They always meet us at the door and search what we're carrying, before we can go in. It's the same for everybody, just routine, but it always makes me feel guilty. As if they think we'd be trying to smuggle in something dangerous. As if we'd be looking for some way around the rules.

The thing is, we don't even realize sometimes, my wife and I. What counts as dangerous, I mean. We learned the obvious things early on—they made us take Dee Dee's ceramic Far Side mug back home with us, that first day, and the instant coffee we brought her had to be poured into a margarine tub, from the glass jar. Those things made sense, once they were explained to us. Glass and ceramic, you could smash them and come up with a ragged edge. Dee Dee asked us for a jump rope, because they wouldn't let her go outside alone to run or even walk, for exercise; we went to the sports store and bought one of those high-tech ropes, with wood handles and a strap at the center to balance the weight. When we presented it for inspection, it got checked with the other sharps.

A *jump rope*? I said, and the nurse didn't have to tell me why, because Helen caught on right away, and she said *Honey* to me and then I got it, too: you could hang yourself with this toy. The thought of it pulled something sharp inside my gut and with the pull came a picture of my daughter, double-jumping between her best friends in the street we lived on, her hair bouncing in a braid. *Down in the valley where the green grass grows, there sat Dee Dee as pretty as a rose.*

Our daughter's bed is the middle one in a room of three. She faces the window when she sleeps, and on the door of the standing closet she has taped the get-well cards her friends sent her, sympathetic Snoopys and teddy bears, the messages inside signed with X's and O's. At first I thought she wouldn't want to tell anybody she was here, but my wife thinks it's healthy, she shouldn't be ashamed. "What if she was in with a broken leg?" Helen asked me. "She needs help, Tom. It's nothing we have to hide." Still, I sense that she shares my discomfort at having people know. This is a psychiatric unit, not a hospital for bones or blood. What's in traction is my daughter's soul.

She has been here a week now, and unless they discharge her sooner than they expect to, she will still be here on her birthday, her twenty-fourth. Last year we all marked the twenty-third by going to a Red Sox game, Dee Dee and her brother—our son, Dan—Dee Dee's boyfriend Edward, and Helen and I. The Red Sox won that night, and Dee Dee and Edward got engaged. Dee Dee called it a triple play, all those things to celebrate at the same time.

They were married in December, and they moved to an apartment in town, close to the law school, where they met in Torts. It's not a great neighborhood—it borders the poorest section of the city, and I told Dee Dee from the beginning that I was worried about her, walking home at night from the library alone. She said they would try to study together, and most of the time they did.

But on the thirtieth of April, a week ago, Edward was playing softball with other men from their class, and he joined them afterward for beer at the Pour House, across from the playing field. Dee Dee worked in the library until nine o'clock, past sunfall, and then she gathered up her books in the leather backpack I gave her for Christmas; her load is always heavy, it weighs a ton, but she is strong, she can carry it all.

She stopped at the convenience store for a frozen dinner,

and then began to walk down the long block, toward the apartment. When she was halfway there, a man stepped out of the alley behind the laundromat, and asked her for a light. When she said she didn't have one, he moved behind her in a single motion she couldn't follow, a flash of dark she felt rather than saw; he tore the backpack away from her and threw it in the Dumpster, with a curse. Then he grabbed her by the wrists and leaned her against the laundromat's brick wall, lifting a rough hand to her mouth. She tasted salt and dirt on the skin of his fingers, and she smelled wet cotton and sweat.

If she could have spoken, she would have told him that she wouldn't scream, couldn't find her voice in all that fear, but he didn't let her. He kept the hand over her lips and nose as he slid her down to the cement and lay her back, putting the frozen dinner under her head for a pillow. *Relax*, he told her, and when she laughed, so did he. But after the laugh she couldn't breathe because he was blocking her air, and she passed out, then came to sometime later, when he was finishing. He hoisted his body off hers and she couldn't even tell at first that he had separated himself, because she still felt his weight, still felt the heat and rip of being split open at the seam. He ran off, and she gathered herself together, righting her clothes, testing her legs before she put them one in front of the other until she reached home.

This is what she told the police, after Edward returned to find her shaking under the covers, sucking her thumb. She had showered and dressed in a nightgown and put her clothes through the wash. She tried to convince him that nothing was the matter, she was just feeling sick, that she was anxious about exams. But he didn't believe her, and finally she told him that she had been raped. Edward began to breathe hard, the way he does after running, and he tried to put his arm around her, but she was sitting in a position that wouldn't allow this, knees up, arms locked in a shrug. She began rocking a little, and Edward got scared. He called the police though she made him promise he wouldn't, and then he called us. When the police got there, she didn't talk until they brought in a woman officer.

Helen and Edward and I waited in the small living room, and I read the titles of books on the shelf behind my son-in-law's shoulder: *Fit for Life, Presumed Innocent, Ascent of Man*. Then I read them backwards (*efiL rof tiF*) to keep my mind at work.

They brought her to the hospital—we followed, Edward driving, forgetting to brake until the last moment at every light—and into an examining room for questions and for tests. Helen tapped the thigh of her jeans with a tin ashtray, and Edward sat with the heels of his hands against his forehead, looking down at his feet. He was still wearing his softball clothes, shorts and sneakers, and a T-shirt from their honeymoon at Palm Beach. There were no books to read, so I concentrated on the TV bolted to a corner of the wall. It was tuned to "The Honeymooners," and when I laughed at something Ed Norton did, Helen said, "Stop, Tom," and I remembered with a shock why we were there.

After a while the policewoman came out with the doctor, who was also a woman, and they sat down with us, both of them trying to smile.

"Is she all right?" Helen said, and I could tell the words had been dammed up in her throat.

"Well, yes," the doctor said.

"What does that mean?" Edward asked her. "What do you mean by *well*?" Though he is a small man, a boy really, he was ready to fight; I saw his fists closing, but then the vein in his neck gave away what he really wanted to do, which was cry.

"Well, we're a little confused." The doctor brushed her hand across the clipboard she held, as if gathering to show us in her fingers what her study of Dee Dee had found. "She has all the psychological symptoms of having been raped—a classic reaction, in fact. The trauma is very real. But her medical condition isn't consistent with the assault she described."

"What does that mean?" Edward asked, again. Helen

tossed the ashtray like a frisbee onto the table, and the doctor, who was looking down, jumped.

"What are you telling us?" Helen said.

This time it was the officer who answered. "We can't be sure, but it's possible she wasn't actually aware of what happened, if she was passed out," she said. "She feels brutalized—that's clear—but there isn't any physical evidence of rape. Or of *any* sexual encounter in quite a while, is that right?" She was checking with the doctor, who nodded, looking down again.

The rest of us turned to look at Edward. "Oh, for God's sake," he said. "We've both been tired. It's exam time. Besides, she hasn't been into it, lately." He reached back to rub his neck, and made the sound between his lips that meant he was embarrassed. "I can't believe I'm talking about this."

Helen was brushing her hair. She does this when she's nervous, takes the brush out of her purse at the most irrelevant times—when she's driving, at a funeral, in the grocery store. Her hair never needs it, but she does it anyway, attacks it in long hard strokes until her scalp must tingle from the heat of the bristles, and the brush looks like a nest.

"There's something you're not saying," she said to the doctor and the policewoman. "Tell us what it is."

The two women looked at each other to decide who would answer; the doctor gave it with her eyes to the cop, who said, "We think it's possible that for some reason, she made a false report."

"You mean *lied*?" Edward shot up out of his chair, and almost fell over from the force of his outrage. "What the hell are you saying?" He began coughing, and I held his shoulders until he stopped.

"She would never do that," I told them. "It has to be true."

Then Dee Dee was there with us, standing at the edge of the waiting room, gripping the wall, accompanied by a nurse who spotted her with arms half-lifted, ready to catch her if she fell. "Honey," Helen said, and went to her, and I followed, but our daughter halted us with a raised and trembling palm. Behind us, Edward coughed again, and the sound made Dee Dee wince, her eyes remote and lightless in her flat white face.

"They're right," she said, and it was the voice of my six-year-old daughter, who came to our bedroom one morning and woke Helen and me to confess she had stolen a piece of Beechnut gum from the pack on my bureau. "There was no man tonight; I made him up." Now, as then, she was waiting to be punished. "I'm sorry."

Her birthday falls on a Wednesday, and by noontime I still haven't decided what to get for her. The stakes feel so high I am afraid of fumbling, of offering the wrong thing. Helen has bought and wrapped many gifts from us together, for this occasion—more than any other birthday or Christmas of the past, as if we could build with all the packages a fortress against the danger looking for entrance to our daughter's mind. But I always like to give a remembrance that's just from me, and walking back to the office from lunch, I pass the window at Snyder's and have a brainstorm. This is where I bought the leather backpack for Dee Dee at Christmastime, and when I go inside I find one identical to the original gift, and on my way into my building, carrying the bag, something else occurs to me. On the phone, to Helen, I say, "What about the backpack? She said the guy threw it in the Dumpster. If she was wrong, does that mean she still has it?"

This is how we speak of that night, to each other: we use words like *upset* instead of *crazy, wrong* instead of *lie.* Helen—who keeps losing weight in her voice and body, all her energy used up in fretting, trying to figure this thing out—sighs and says she doesn't know, she doesn't know, so I call Edward and ask him, and he says no, the police did find it in the garbage, and I say, How can that be? and he says he doesn't know, either. I suggest that this may be a clue in support of Dee Dee's story, and Edward reminds me that she admitted it was a lie.

"I hate that word," I tell him, and he says, "What do you want me to say?" I can almost hear him shrugging, into the phone. He is trying to keep up with classes—Dee Dee thought she'd be able to, too, studying with the notes he copied for her, planning to ask for passes from the hospital to take her exams—but she gave up the first week and applied for Incompletes, and though Edward swears he will not, he may have to do the same. Usually we go at different times to see her, because the doctors recommend short and separate visits, so I don't know how things have been between Edward and Dee Dee, whether they suffer the same silences as Helen and Dan and I when it is our turn, or whether she has been able to explain anything to her husband in a way he can understand.

But tonight we are all going together, to celebrate her birthday. Edward meets us at our house and we drive together in my car, Dan and Edward in the back, as if our family has always had two sons instead of a son and a daughter. The wrapped gifts slide between them on the seat when we take the corners. Dan is struggling to make conversation with his brother-in-law, who is only two years older; they have always been easy with each other, but this situation strains them, with the threats and questions it implies. I have the impression that Dan suspects Edward of something, and feels guilty because of it. Catching my son's eyes in the rearview mirror, I shift in my place behind the wheel and open the window to let air in, so the sweat on my back can breathe.

The hospital is a small one, private, spread out among a few low buildings around a pretty lawn; it looks like a prep school or a little college, dorms hugging the quad, except that the dorms are filled with hospital beds and therapy offices, and carry soothing names like Green Cottage and Sage Hall. There is no fence or gate to pass through, only a row of shrubs separating confinement from free will. Driving in, I feel relieved that I kept her on my policy last year, so she would be eligible for this good and gentle care.

Everything here depends on your privileges, or what the initiated call "privs": whether you can leave the unit at all, how often, for how long, and with whom. Privs aren't issued as reward or punishment, the nurse on duty explained to us when Dee Dee was admitted. They are determined by how "safe" the staff thinks you are, and how much responsibility you can be trusted with, mostly for yourself.

"What the hell does *safe* mean?" I remember asking. Helen and I were standing with the nurse in a corner of the unit lounge, which is like a living room, four couches in a square around a coffee table, and a TV at one end. Edward and Dee Dee were going through her suitcase with a counselor, separating out the things she could conceivably hurt herself with: they took custody of her hair dryer, her compact mirror, notebooks with wire spirals.

"Most of the people who come here have been self-destructive at some point," the nurse told us.

"You mean suicidal?" Helen said. In the car on the way over she'd made me stop, telling me she had to vomit, but nothing happened, and I thought she might be bringing it up now.

"Sometimes, but not necessarily," the nurse said. Her name was Joanne, and she looked even younger than Dee Dee. She didn't wear a uniform, but instead had on a sundress over a T-shirt with rolled sleeves. Her arms were tan already, this early in the season, and I guessed she had been on vacation in the last month, someplace warm, with someone who loved her. "A lot of sexually abused women cut themselves with a razor or a knife. On their arms, mostly, or sometimes on their legs." She watched us react and then paused, like a teacher waiting for her students to catch up in their notes. "The internal pain is so intense that it gives them a distraction, and relief, to feel something physical instead."

"But Dee Dee said she wasn't raped," Helen said, and the words seemed to choke her.

I took her hand, which was shockingly cold, and reminded her, "We don't know what happened."

"Well." Joanne looked as if she wanted to smile at us, for comfort, but decided halfway into the gesture that it wasn't the right one. "She'll be able to talk about it in therapy." She reached out to pat Helen's sleeve, and I waited to be touched too, but at that moment the counselor brought Dee Dee over with the searched suitcase, and we had to say good-bye. Edward hung back and waited for us to finish, pretending to watch TV. We would have hugged her, but they had already advised us of the hospital rule against personal contact, so I lifted my fingertips to my lips and kissed them, then turned them to my daughter in a kind of salute, hoping she would know how much I wanted it to mean. When she picked up the suitcase to bring it to her room, I stole a look up and down her arms, to check for scars, and I noticed Helen doing the same thing; our eyes met in relief when we saw the flesh intact, and on our way out to the car we gripped each other around the waist, tightly, digging our nails in, until it hurt.

After two weeks, Dee Dee's privileges allow her only as far as the building's basement, which is divided into three rooms for visiting, laundry, and ping-pong. The social room contains sofas like the ones in the upstairs lounge; candy and soda machines; and shelves of books people have donated, copies of Shakespeare plays and old Western Civ texts with the pages falling out. It's here, on the white tile floor, that Dee Dee jumps rope and does some calisthenics, when she can get one of the counselors to supervise. The image of my grown daughter playing a child's game alone, in the cellar of what is essentially a loony bin, makes me want to hide and scream and punch a wall down, all at the same time. *Along came Somebody and kissed her on the nose.* ("Somebody" always changed, a different boy's name every time I heard it sung to the slap of the rope against the sidewalk.) *How many kisses did she get?*

And it is here that we will have her party, in the circle of seats around the low table scarred with graffiti, DR. FLEMBAG SUCKS and PLEASE HELP ME engraved in light scratches across the cheap blond wood. How did they get there, with the sharp edges under guard? Perhaps fingernails, I think; perhaps the end of a ballpoint or a hair pin. The desperation, the ingenuity it took to leave these messages, amazes and frightens me.

Helen sets the party things down on top of the blemishes, precisely enough that I know she has aimed to cover them. There is a cake, of course, with a sugar *24* rising from the center; Helen baked it last night, in the pan shaped like a heart, which she bought for one Valentine's Day when the kids were little, and hadn't used since because the batter stuck to the sides, and fell apart when she tried to turn it out. For this cake, she sat at the kitchen table after it came from the oven, and worked a knife around the heart's cooled edges to make sure it wouldn't cling.

She pulls out cups and plates and napkins, all of the same festive confetti design; but her fingers move slowly in setting the table, as if this were the grimmest of tasks. Edward stacks the presents at an end of the couch and then sits next to them, drumming the one on top with bitten fingers. He doesn't believe Dee Dee needs to be here, and it shows.

I pour soda into the cups and offer some to Dee Dee, who is watching all of this, all of us, with the expression of someone observing a foreign rite. "Does it have caffeine?" she asks, taking the drink from me, looking into the soda as if it might answer her. "I won't be able to sleep tonight, if it does."

I turn the bottle around so she can see the label, CAFFEINE FREE, and I can't help adding, "We know, honey. They told us," to which she says, "Sorry." Helen gives me a dirty look, and I say, "No, *I* am" to my daughter, and put out a hand to touch her arm; but she pulls it back with such a jerk that the soda spills.

"No personal contact, Dad," she says, her voice vibrating with the fear of being caught.

"There's nobody watching," I tell her.

"I don't care."

She is shaking; it is like the times she used to come out

of the water at the Cape, shivering as a cloud passed, heading for the towel Helen held open to her. Dee Dee would disappear in the terrycloth, burrowing in for dryness and warmth, until all I could see were her wet braids hanging over the side. When the hair dried and she took the braids out, she looked like a miniature woman, her small face framed by a billow of brown kinks that caught the sky's light and made her eyes in her sun-dark skin appear faded and wise.

"Honey," Helen says, pausing as she places the candles in the frosting, "what's wrong?"

But the shaking stops as Dee Dee smiles at her brother, who is standing behind me. Dan has been in the ping-pong room, blowing up balloons, and now he brings them in on a crepe paper streamer, which he tapes between the walls so the colors bob like a rubber buoy on the ceiling. He sets his portable cassette player on the table and turns it on, and "I Feel Good" comes out of the plastic speaker, James Brown sounding hollow but happy as he tries to set the mood.

Dan lip-syncs into a pretend microphone and picks up his sister's hand; she has begun moving even before they are partnered, dancing with her shoulders leading, all beauty and breeze in a slow shimmy. Always our son and daughter danced with each other like this, from the time before they were in school. There is a rhythm between them that they both understand, and they never had to learn how to move this way, just knew it from the beginning, and when they are around a lot of people they always attract attention, because it looks so easy when they do it, so graceful and so good. At Dee Dee and Edward's wedding, the groom and I both had to cut in on the bride and her brother, because they stole so many dances together. This birthday party is an echo of that day, Edward and I watching stupidly from the sidelines, while Helen looks on with what I can tell is a proud and hopeful heart; and only I can tell, when she turns her face away from our dancing children, that she has begun to cry. I know I should do something to comfort her, but I can't think what, and somehow I believe that whatever I might try now would only make it worse.

By the time the song is over, Helen's tears are, too, and she can smile as Dee Dee gives Dan a hug that would embarrass many men his age, close and tight around his neck, her face in the shoulder of his shirt. He stands firm with his arms supporting his sister, and does not try to escape. Edward looks jealous of Dan for knowing what to do. When Dan and Dee Dee finally separate, they look at the rest of us as if they have just emerged from a cave to be greeted by more rescuers than they expected. "Surprise," Helen says, because Dee Dee appears so dazed, and our daughter laughs almost too strongly, but maybe it is only because we are in a hospital that the force of her laughter stings.

"What about the personal contact?" I ask, trying to look as if I am only pretending to feel rejected. Dan and Dee Dee are still so close to each other that their elbows touch as they bend to pick up the pieces of cake Helen cut after we turned the cassette volume down for the birthday song.

"Well, it doesn't apply to Dan, because he isn't really a person," Dee Dee says, and she laughs again, her mouth a dark oval of chocolate. Dan lets her teasing pass with only a smile, and I look at Helen to see if she realizes the same thing I do, that our children are grown-ups; but from her face I sense that maybe this happened a long time ago, and I just didn't know.

"Twenty-four years ago today," Helen says, announcing the beginning of a familiar monologue as she presses triangular holes in the Hawaiian Punch can. She will not drink soda, and she always tried to discourage it in the kids, but only Dan would follow her in this. Dee Dee had a sweet tooth from the start, which I fed when Helen wasn't looking; we ate candy bars and Cokes from the refrigerator in the basement, next to the washer and dryer, where I have a worktable, and where I make things out of wood. When Dan was a baby I bought him a toy tool set, but he always dropped the hammer when I put it in his hand, and it was Dee Dee I would find playing with the plastic screws and wrenches, concentrating on some close task, tongue set between her teeth.

By the time she was five she was helping me shape things, her small hands piggy-backing mine as they sent boards through the lathe. We worked on weekends, mostly, building furniture for the house—a toy chest, a fireplace bench, a hutch for the dining room—and one winter we made a set of animals, and an ark to put them in. I had suggested a barn, but Dee Dee was in Sunday School then; she liked the story of the covenant, and she was born loving the rain. We would climb the stairs from our Saturday sessions trailing sawdust from our shoes, and at supper Helen couldn't understand why we weren't eating, because she didn't know about the peanut butter cups whose wrappers we wadded into basketballs and shot at the washer's mouth, then retrieved in a single fistful of foil so Helen wouldn't find the evidence in the next load. Dee Dee still takes after me, carrying a can of Coke with her to every class the way I always have one open on my desk at work. Helen has long since given up trying to reform us; she just looks the other way.

"Twenty-four years ago *today*," she repeats, emphasizing the importance of what she wants to say. "I was lying in the maternity ward at Hale Hospital, holding my new baby and waiting for her father to show up." This is a variation on the story she tells every year on this day, always without the preface that Dee Dee arrived in the world two weeks early, while I was on a training trip in Huntsville, Alabama, learning the things I needed to know to work at the company that had just hired me. Helen hadn't wanted me to go, but I had no choice; and for twenty-four years now she has taken pleasure in telling the story of our daughter's birth as if I had something better to do while it was happening.

"There was a woman in the next bed whose baby was born dead the day before I had Dee Dee," she goes on, and I see Dan and Dee Dee and even Edward—who has heard the story only twice—move a little in surprise, as I do, because this is not a part of the routine we know.

"How come you never told us that before?" Dee Dee asks her.

Helen says, "Well, it always seemed too sad. She didn't stay long after I got there, but it was long enough for her to see me with *my* baby. Her husband was there, too." She pauses to let this last fact rub itself into me. "They both couldn't stop looking at Dee Dee—like they were mesmerized. I offered to let them hold her, and the mother didn't want to, but the father came over and took you for a while—" she addresses Dee Dee directly—"and he sang you a song, and it broke my heart; you could tell he had gotten ready to sing it to his own."

"What was it?" Dee Dee asks, sounding desperate to have this piece of information, as if without knowing so, she has been seeking it all her life.

"Oh, I don't remember. Some little song I never heard before. For all I know, he made it up. But it was sweet. I remember thinking I would have cried, if I hadn't been so tired." Helen pauses again, and her eyes are focused not on the room we are in or the people around her, but on the lullaby sung to her baby so many years ago, a song that will always be lost because she has forgotten it, and because Dee Dee was too new to make sense of anything.

Though the story is a sad one, I feel silly anger at this distant, grieving man, who held my daughter before I did. It takes longer than it should for me to realize that Dee Dee is crying now, and has been, since before her mother stopped talking; she sits between Dan and Edward, and Dan puts his hand over his sister's, but Edward looks afraid to touch her, as if he is not sure what effect it will have. I wonder if I am the only one of us who notices him shifting in his corner of the couch, his body turning almost imperceptibly away from Dee Dee, his shoulders bulky with the weight of what they have been forced, these last weeks, to carry.

Helen watches Dee Dee for a moment, and I expect her

to go to her, or to say something that will soothe. Instead, inexplicably—alarmingly—she continues telling the story. "I didn't want to ask if their baby had been a boy or a girl, but I was dying to know. After the mother got transferred, the nurse told me. It was a girl, and it looked okay when it first came out, but then they saw it wasn't moving. I guess they slapped her and did all the stuff you're supposed to, but she never took a breath."

If Helen's plan was to stop Dee Dee's crying, it's working; for some reason, as her mother talks, my daughter settles down, her breath sounding more regular, the tears pooling in her eyes. "They didn't even live around here, the couple," Helen concludes, as if delivering a punchline. "They were in town for a wedding, and her water broke at the church. They were from somewhere in Virginia, I remember. Something Falls."

This nonending is the end of the story, and in response Dee Dee presses her hand against her chest as at the end of a scary movie, and she nods once and tries to smile, and reaches for her plate of cake and her soda cup, which she drains in a gulp. I look at Dan and Edward, to see if they get any of this, but I can tell they don't, either. Finally Dan lifts his hand in front of his face, the imaginary microphone again at his lips.

"Hailing from Something Falls, Virginia, our contestant enjoys doing nothing at all, except when she is doing something else," he says in the tone of a game show host, and his inflection is so right it makes us all laugh, and Dan looks relieved and a little proud of himself. Dee Dee leans forward to cut herself another piece of the cake, and behind our party another patient, a girl about Dee Dee's age, passes through the room with a pile of laundry. We fall silent as she goes by, each of us watching her without being obvious about it; she says "hi" like any normal person, and I find myself looking for signs of what landed her in a hospital like this.

Dee Dee must realize we are all wondering, because she explains to us, when the girl is safely in the next room, that she is an anorexic who pores over *Gourmet* and *Bon Appetit* before bedtime each night, ripping out photographs of desserts to tape next to her bed. She goes on to tell us other stories she has learned while living here: about the teenager who cuts the shapes of flowers into her flesh; about the woman diagnosed as a multiple personality, who resents the other patients and staff when they can't tell her identities apart, though they all reside in the same body.

"What she needs is an unlimited supply of HELLO-MY-NAME-IS tags," Dan suggests. "Or she could wear one of those memo boards you just wipe off, when you want to change what it says."

"Wait—I know," Dee Dee adds, inspired, "how about one of those signs like you see in the record store. Now Playing: Jennifer. Next Up: Bernadette."

We are all laughing (and a voice in my head reassures me: see, we can laugh, we can laugh) when the anorexic girl walks through our room again, carrying the detergent she will have to check back into sharps. She looks at us with a smile of puzzlement, and I realize that there is probably not often the sound of pleasure in this place.

"Would you like some cake?" I ask without thinking, and across from me my daughter takes in her breath, a warning too late.

"No thank you," the other girl says, her answer automatic, resolute. Her lips, I see now, are like ghost skin, pale and papery, trapping hunger and a shriek. As she continues out to the hallway, we watch her become smaller and darker in the shadow of the stairs. Her legs under her shorts are bowed and thin as tomato stakes, and her spine shows through her shirt.

"Jesus," Edward says. He tosses his plate, with half his piece left, onto the vandalized table. The abruptness of the gesture and the pitch of his voice make the rest of us stop chewing and look around, as if we have all just awakened to find ourselves in a place other than where we went to sleep. "What are we doing here, Dee Dee?" he says, and now he can touch her hand, lean closer to speak in her ear, his face next to the hair that smells like honey.

Instead of answering, she feeds him a bite from her fork. When he makes a face before he swallows, she asks him, "Is it too sweet for you?"

The next morning, we get a phone call early. Helen and I are both dressing for work; I am still a little breathless and cloudy from the dream I was having when the alarm went off, which I remembered distinctly and with dread for the few minutes before I got up, and then forgot in the first motions of the day, except that Dee Dee and I were in danger, and I was supposed to be able to save us, but I failed.

We have not had sex in a month, since before all this began. Helen doesn't seem to miss it, and I am grateful for this, because I could not touch her if she wanted it, but this way I am not blamed. The subtlest connection of our limbs in bed makes my heart speed up, but not with desire: it is anticipation racing fear. She has not seemed to notice that I feel this way, and I would not be able to tell her why, if she did ask, because I cannot tell myself.

Dee Dee is the one we should be talking about, and we do. But after the first few days there is nothing to say except the same questions over and over, in different groups of words, and finally these fade to silences of frustration and suspense. We have forgone our usual mealtimes together, breakfast and supper, in favor of snacks eaten standing at the kitchen counter or in front of the TV. Dan used to come by often, to do his laundry or to pick up mail that hadn't made it to his new apartment, and before all this he stayed a while, and we talked about his job or the Red Sox or a girl he wanted to date, but since his sister's hospitalization he is only in and out, hurrying to finish his errands, moving through the house the way he would through a post office or a laundromat. He seems reluctant to talk to me or Helen, as if by cutting down on conversation he will reduce the chances of learning something he can't afford to know.

So we get this phone call, the phone call, from the hospital, from the social worker assigned to Dee Dee's case, a Lolly Sheftick, which is enough to make you laugh, except that she doesn't look the way her name sounds, like a crazy grandmother with bad makeup and a wig—in fact she's pretty in a flushed and angled way, taller than Helen and slimmer, but with a smile that includes rather than threatens women less good-looking than she. After all these years of being married, I can tell between the types.

She greets us with the smile on the porch of Green Cottage, where she asked us to meet her when she called, to discuss "a matter of some urgency"—as soon as we could. I asked if it could wait until after work, not that I didn't care about my daughter, but I had a meeting the first thing, and as I asked to put it off I felt my breakfast coming up and had to step away from the phone, which I handed to Helen while I was sick in the sheets.

I used to think of social workers as those women who visited poor people, families with no fathers and crowds of hungry kids. But the social workers at this hospital are the members of the treatment team—each patient has one— whose job it is to handle the "family therapeutic component" of the case. This Lolly Sheftick explains to us outside her office, in a quiet voice around a table strewn with *Good Housekeeping* and *Self*. A plant in the center of the table sheds brown leaves from its pot, and I wonder who is responsible for not taking care of it. Lolly stands, and I expect her to lead Helen and me through the door that shows her name, but instead she puts a hand up like a gentle traffic guard, and says she would like to talk to my wife first, privately, and would I please wait here.

Helen looks at me for some clue, some secret signal, to tell her what this means. I shrug—the movement is spastic, beyond my control, and though I try to repress it, it turns into a twitch. They go behind the door and shut it, and I am alone in the lobby, except for a woman who sits at the reception desk; but she is listening to something through the headset of a dictaphone, so I am, essentially, alone. I locate a wastebasket in the corner, in case I have to be sick again. I read some things in reverse: NO SMOKING PLEASE (ESAELP GNIKOMS ON) and a picnic sign-up sheet from which I realize, with a moment's diversion of amusement and surprise, that "desserts" spelled backwards is "stressed."

But when this moment passes, I remember where I am, and I stand suddenly and the receptionist looks up with a startled motion, a palm flying to her chest. I lift a hand to show her I'm sorry, and on Lolly Sheftick's door I knock with knuckles jerking from the wrist. She opens the door and beyond it in a chair against the wall I see my wife still waiting, still with the question in her eyes, and Lolly Sheftick says, "But Mr. Osborne, we're not ready yet," and I tell her, "Yes, I am.

"I want to hear this," I add. "Please let me in."

"Mrs. Osborne?" Lolly says. "Do you mind if he's here, too?"

"Of course not. He's my husband," Helen says. "Why would I mind?

"You're scaring me," she goes on to caution Lolly. "You'd better tell me why."

There is an empty seat next to Helen, but instead I take the one that makes a triangle among us, and I look at the four feminine legs across from me, both sets crossed at the knee, my wife's tapping the carpet with the toe of her best pumps, the least scuffed, the most appropriate pair to wear to an appointment about your daughter's mental health. We both changed our clothes after we got the phone call, without discussing it. We seemed to realize that what we had on already would not be enough, that we needed to be more than presentable because we were likely to face a trial on charges we had not yet heard.

Lolly Sheftick folds her hands on top of her knee and says, "This is not going to be an easy thing. I asked Dee Dee if she wanted to be here, but she said no. She's probably right, actually. It would probably be too much."

"Are you going to tell us why she said she was raped,

when she wasn't?" Helen, I see, is wrapping her fingers in a grip stronger than prayer.

"Well," Lolly Sheftick says, "we believe it's more complicated than that. No, she wasn't attacked two weeks ago. She's told us that. But her feelings of trauma, her reaction to what she said happened, are as real as if she was. We believe—and we've talked to Dee Dee about this—that she made up the attack almost subconsciously, to explain the feelings she's having now about something that happened long ago."

"Long *ago*?" Helen says, and I watch the grip come apart in her lap.

"When children are abused sexually, they often forget it's happened, even as it's happening. The psyche tells itself, 'You can't tolerate knowing this,' and so the part that knows, the part that experiences it, splits off from the conscious mind." Lolly picks up a pen from her desk and I watch the way she fingers it, and I realize that she smoked at one time, with great appetite, perhaps until recently; she looks very much as if she would like to take a drag.

"Are you telling me my daughter was raped a long time ago?" The words die in the fire of Helen's voice, and then she laughs, and the difference between the two sounds gives them a sense of obscenity. "That's impossible. Impossible. I don't know what you're saying." She looks at me and puts her hand out, palm up in my direction, to show me that it's my turn, now, to object to what she's hearing.

But I have left the office, let myself leave the body that still sits in my place, decided not to listen anymore, chosen to take off. I make a sound that could mean anything. Helen stiffens in her chair. Lolly Sheftick lifts the cap of the pen to her mouth, pulls it between her lips, bites it, then yanks it out through her teeth.

"Mr. Osborne," she says, "this is uncomfortable, I know. It's worse than that. But I have to tell you both that what Dee Dee remembers has to do with you." Though her tone is professional, courteous, trying even to be kind because she can destroy me, I see the light of hate ignite her face, a smoulder moving slowly and heating as it spreads.

"It does," I say, meaning to make it a question, but it doesn't come out that way.

"What?" Helen says. She picks her purse off the floor and begins to rummage for her hairbrush, though she looks not inside the bag but at my hands, which start to dance along the chair arms.

"What, Tom?" she says, locating the brush, and in taking it out she flips a book of matches on the floor. While she waits for me to speak, she presses the packed bristles deep into the soft flesh of her palm, until I can see from her face that she is hurting.

"Stop that," I tell her, frowning at the brush, and I think of reaching over to take it from her, but my hands are still rapping and fluttering at the sidearms of my seat. We watch them, the three of us, including Lolly Sheftick, as if my hands are strange and toxic creatures we don't know how to kill.

Finally, when the hands don't stop jittering, when nobody says a word, Helen leans forward with the brush and slams it down on my fingers, shocking them to rest. Lolly Sheftick giggles—not a long one, she stops as soon as she hears it, but it is enough to make her realize she shouldn't have, and she says "I'm sorry" with chagrin.

"What happens now?" I ask, after a moment when none of us seems to know. Outside the room someone is swearing at the copying machine. On Lolly's desk there is a photograph of her and someone else, but it is too small to see distinctly, and I resist the urge to squint or lean to make out the details.

"Wait a minute," Helen says, still clenching the handle. "What does she remember? What is it about you?" Though she is referring to me, she points the question at Lolly, who when she looks at me sends pity blended with contempt. If I told her this—what I recognize in her face, as she appears to let the blade drop—she would deny the mercy, and claim only her disgust. She would be ashamed to admit compassion for what I'm suffering now.

Yet I know she feels it, the same way I know how Helen's feeling (stomach rubbing itself raw), how the woman at the copier feels, waiting for her page. There are certain things we learn by being human, and one is that we're more alike than we can bear. So Lolly Sheftick pretends she can't imagine what's inside me, as she invites me to respond.

"Mr. Osborne?" she asks.

But when she sees me spinning, she tells Helen herself. "Dee Dee remembers being abused by her father," she says, the words emerging at a slow, distorted speed. "I'm sorry, Mrs. Osborne. I wish it weren't true."

"Oh, for God's sake," Helen says. "Don't be ridiculous." She actually seems to smile. "I'm so sick of this abuse talk, it's everywhere you go. Abuse, abuse. How come you never used to hear that word? It's the latest thing. A fad, like sushi."

I wait for Lolly to laugh again, but instead she looks disturbed. I watch us from a corner of the ceiling, where I'm hanging from a nerve.

"I understand your reaction," she tells Helen, "because we see it all the time. You don't want to believe it. Neither does Dee Dee. But her memories are real." Abruptly, she tosses the pen onto her blotter, opens the desk drawer and pulls out a cigarette from a pack of Merits, which she lights with the urgency of a swimmer sucking air.

"She feels them in her body," Lolly says, turning her head to exhale toward the wall above her desk, at the buzzer labeled EMERGENCY (if I rush by her and press it, will we all be saved?). "She's re-experiencing the sensations, as if they're happening to her now. It's not unusual. I'm sorry," she says again, dragging for dear life.

She looks at me. "Do you have anything you want to say, Mr. Osborne? I realize this is . . . ." But there is no language for what this is, and she can see it in my face. When I start to speak, I choke on my own swallow, and cough to clear my throat.

Helen is waiting, her breath suspended, her body taut with dread. "I didn't abuse her," I tell them, and my wife's release is audible, the sound I hear in bed. Before she can turn it into words, I head her off and whisper, "I wouldn't call it that."

How do these things happen? How can you understand? It's not that I forgot, like Dee Dee—although they say she didn't, either, not the way you forget the name of someone you hardly know, or what you ate last Wednesday. These are unimportant facts, the ones you can afford to lose in order to have room for what you need, the vital contents of the head and heart and the machinery between them, what makes you who you are.

No, I remember all the nights, the darkness of her room, the way the walls held us in comfort, cozy, when it was cold outside. And in summer, with the windows open, how the air would touch us through the screen, and I would lift the sheet across her shoulder and watch her fall to sleep.

When it began, she welcomed me, her body making barely a dimple in the big-girl bed. I felt such love for her, such wonder; and as I swept her hair behind the soft part of her ear, she closed her eyes and smiled. We played a game with words, "Dee Dee" and "Daddy," whispering them to each other until the syllables got twisted and the names became nonsense. We called it tucking in. I was gentle with my hands, and from the first they were electri-fied by the sensation of my cheek against her skin.

There was no sin in it, to start with. Then the awe I felt at what she let me do, and the sweet salve of her laugh, out-roared the "no" I knew I should be heeding; I looked into her face and saw the light there, the smile and the trust, and I changed them because I could, no other reason. I saw that I would leave a mark as deep as death and so I did it, and with the mark made evil out of love. I know it and, God help me, knew it then, but only the way you know a thing in theory, with other people's proofs at the back of the book. You look them up and see how they arrived there, and you know the answers to be true; but at the test it goes out of your head, you are back to your own sad way of figuring, and you forget what you swore to yourself you would understand in time.

In the mornings it woke with me. Not as far back as the little bed, but the moments after, when I went down the hall and in to Helen, who slept with one arm dangling, pointing at the floor. I felt like a burglar in that passage, an intruder in my home, come to steal something that would not be reported missing because it was invisible, and because no one knew how valuable it had been. Once I opened my eyes, I sent my memory of the night to lodge in a place other than conscience, which was filled up long ago. Even so, at breakfast, I waited for my daughter to turn her head from me, and it always took me by surprise when she would plop a kiss against my forehead and ask me how I was.

Now, they tell me why: during the nights, after I left her, a cloud spread through her senses, wiping out my visits and waking her in white. Until this spring, when something—was it the thaw? her class on criminals? a movement Edward made above her in the bed?—blew aside the vapors, and left the truth exposed.

It stopped when she was twelve. She got her period that year, and when Helen came to tell me, looking proud and brave (I think she had been crying), I was down in the basement building Dee Dee a new bureau, sanding off the boards. My wife held a basket of laundry, a mix of dirty clothes from all the hampers, our underwear with the kids' gymsuits, the dust rags and the towels. She set the load on top of the washer to leave her arms free for a hug, and when I held her in it, our bodies fitting flush so nothing could have come between them, I heard, "She's not my baby anymore," and I swear to God I couldn't tell which one of us had said it. When we pulled apart, I felt as if I had just been shaken out of a long, long dream.

Later, when Dee Dee came down to inspect the bureau, I offered her candy and she took it, watching me while she ate; when I finished mine I crunched the wrapper up and threw it at the open washer, the way we used to, but she folded hers in half and dropped it in the trash bucket, where it fell without a sound. She ran her fingers over the drawers and showed me where they needed smoothing. She told me which varnish she wanted me to use. When Helen called us for supper, she waited until I went up the steps first, instead of letting me follow her, as I always had before.

That night I fell asleep with my arms around Helen, and I woke a few hours later with a jolt, thinking I had been caught, until I remembered that I belonged there, and that I wouldn't have to leave. When I realized that I expected to find myself in a bed that I had soiled, I felt more guilt than after any time with Dee Dee, and I got up and went to her doorway, where I stood and watched her sleep.

She lay curled in an impossibly small space at the edge of the mattress, and her thumb was in her mouth. Her hair drew half a curtain over the hooded eyes. She was the baby we set to nap in a laundry basket, prone on a pillow, wrapped in my flannel shirt. She was easy to carry that way, and it was all we could afford. That first summer, we took her everywhere with us—to the Esplanade for fireworks, to the beach, even to Fenway Park, where she slept until the fifth. She seldom cried, and she outgrew Helen's hugs before any of her friends could bear to let their mothers from their sight. On the playground, when she fell, she froze in landing, and we waited for the wail. But before Helen or I or another grown-up could move to comfort her, she got up to kiss herself on the injury—the finger or the foot—and smearing the tears out of her eyes, she joined the game again.

When she began to change positions in the bed I turned from the doorway, not wanting to be seen, and behind me my son was standing, with his finger on the light. He switched it off and the hall went dark, turning us to shadows. "What's up, Dad?" Danny said, and I could feel him wanting to believe what I would say.

"Just checking," I told him, and I sent him back to bed.

But I saw him waiting by his window, hugging his long arms, until I left his sister's door. The next day I bought him the trumpet he'd been wanting, and bought him lessons, and he was happy, making noise.

Maybe it's foolish, a superstition, but I wonder if it might mean something to Dee Dee, she might say she'd talk to me, if I brought some candy, like in the old days, to the hospital with me. I haven't seen her since her birthday, and Helen will only speak to me on the phone, and only barely, after the day in Lolly Sheftick's office, which was a week ago. When Helen started to lose control that morning, Lolly took her to another room, and I stood to make them think I would go back to the lounge; but when they had left I shut the door behind them, and sat down at Lolly's desk. The photograph I had tried to get a look at, earlier, was propped against the wall. It was a picture of Lolly and a man, in summer, their arms around each other's bathing suit waists, her head against his chest. It was like the one taken of me and Helen at the Cape the week after our wedding, when we were fat and pale with love.

That shot was black and white, and this was color, but there was a common expression in all four faces, a confidence in smiles reflected by the sun. The last time I saw the picture in our album—we were showing it to Edward, the night they got engaged—he said, "Who's that?" and when I, who was turning the pages, didn't answer right away, Helen looked over to see where he was pointing, and she said, "That's us," and I could tell she knew I hadn't recognized myself, and she was not surprised.

On Friday, after work, I drive back to the motel where I've been staying, and change my clothes, and get a dinner at the drive-thru of the Burger King on the way to the hospital, and when I get there I park on the far side of the lot, and eat the dinner, waiting for my family to show up. Visiting hours begin at five-thirty, and at six Helen and Dan arrive together, and they go into Sage Hall. A few minutes later Dee Dee comes outside with them, and they walk to a cluster of wood chairs in the center of the lawn, where the sun makes a circle like a spotlight on a stage. I watch them talking; they even dare to laugh. Then Dan picks up a stick from the ground and begins jabbing it at the grass, until Helen tells him to stop it; I can see reproach in her face, but when he drops the stick, she leans over to touch his knee with fingers she kissed first.

I think about getting out and going over, but I am not even supposed to be here. Helen's made that plain. I imagine sentries in the turrets, poised to shoot on sight. Instead I sit there with the window rolled down, biting the straw from my milkshake until it flakes off in my mouth. When somebody walks by, I put my hand over my forehead, as if rubbing out an ache. When the coast is clear I look over at the three of them, my wife and children saying words I cannot hear. Dan shakes his head a lot, and Dee Dee's face looks old across the distance.

Helen does much of the talking, and at the end of the visit, when they stand and head back to the hall, she puts a hand on each child's shoulder, and leaves it as they walk. They are passing near my car, though I know they won't notice it, because they don't look to the sides as they move forward, just keep on going straight, not because there is nothing to appreciate around these grounds but because there is too much that my daughter needs permission to see and touch and feel.

When they are beyond me and almost to the door, I press my horn a couple of times, trying not to sound frantic, before they can disappear. Dee Dee jumps at the first toot, and at the second all three of them turn around to stare. Then Dan and Dee Dee look at Helen, to see what they should do. I put my head out and say "Hey, hi," and Dee Dee is the first to answer.

"Oh, Daddy," she says to me.

But no one makes a move until I ask, "Will you guys come here a minute? I'm not going to get out," and cautiously they all move toward me, like hunters advancing on hurt and hostile prey.

"You're not supposed to be here," Helen says.

"I know. But I wanted to see you. Thanks for coming," I tell them, as if my car is a cocktail party and they have just arrived. "Where's Edward?" I ask then, to get things rolling.

"He's not here," Dee Dee says.

"I see that."

Dan kicks the tire and flicks the hood with his finger and says, "Look, what do you want?"

"Nothing," I say. His anger scares me. A breeze blows by, and the smell of my burger carton comes up from the car floor to make me queasy.

"Then get out of here," Dan says.

"Can I talk to Dee Dee?"

Helen laughs, exhaling bitterly. "You've got to be kidding."

"What, Dad?" My daughter takes a step forward and pulls her hair around her face. "Tell me."

They are all waiting for what I have to say. But I've forgotten what it was, or if I even knew. "Sorry," I mumble, meaning that I'm lost, but Dan takes it for something else.

"Sorry?" he says. "You're sorry?" He laughs, then spits across the pavement, a sour shooting phlegm.

"That's not what I meant," I tell him, but he will not understand.

"You'd better go," my wife advises. She touches Dee Dee's elbow from behind and Dee Dee tenses, then smiles at her mother so she won't take offense.

"Okay," I say, and start the engine. The smell of food and the force of my family's feelings are squeezing out my breath. I lose contorl of the clutch and the car sputters, and looking up to turn the key again I see my son making a face, as if he knows he could expect no more of me.

"Wait," Dee Dee says, putting a hand out. I shift to neutral, trying not to flinch. She leans into the car and Dan wants to pull her back—I can see him moving—but Helen catches him in time.

My daughter's face is at my level, her eyes mimicking mine. "I'm going to be okay, you know," she tells me. I nod a little foolishly, and drive away confused. Did she mean to give me comfort? Or claim a victory?

We used to have a date on weekend mornings. We made clandestine trips to the bakery, before even Dan was up to watch cartoons, and we never told anyone about our secret, about the pastries we ate on the way home and the Cokes we drank with them. The men in the bakery had a game, pretending week to week that they'd forgotten Dee Dee's name, and when they saw her coming they went into their routine, calling out "Irene!" and "Mildred!" to see how she'd respond.

At first, when she was little, she laughed and shook her head; sometimes she giggled at an odd or ugly name. They knew, of course, and before they gave us our breakfast they said the real one, and she waved a shy good-bye, hugging the warm bag to her chest.

But on the morning that turned out to be our last one there, she wouldn't let them play. She was older then, and instead of picking out a cherry Danish, she asked for a corn muffin with jelly on the side.

"Okay, Lucille," one of the men said, as he reached into the case.

"Tell them my name, Dad," Dee Dee demanded, in a voice I'd never heard from her before.

"They know it, honey." I frowned at her, then smiled at the man and shrugged, to show I couldn't help my kid's behavior.

"Tell them," she said again, and this time both of the men straightened behind the glass display.

"Honey—"

"Tell them," she said, a third time, so close to breaking that the men looked at each other and then at the floured floor. "Tell. Tell. Tell. Tell. Tell. Tell. Tell."

I could feel her breath against my shoulder, and the cool blades of her eyes. Behind us a line was rustling. "Goddammit," I said, slapping a dollar on the counter. "Her name is Deirdre Anne."

"Okay," my daughter said, "let's go," and she took the bag and turned, smiling first at the bakers, then at me, before we went out to the car.

"What's wrong with you?" I said, when we got in.

She was buckling her seatbelt, and her hair fell in her face. "Nothing." Her voice held more, but she contained it; I could see her swallow something down.

We pulled away and I told her, "You embarrassed me back there." She was eating her muffin and she tried to answer, but her throat was thick with crumbs.

"Hey," I said, realizing this was all we'd ended up with. I almost hit the car in front of me, with my hand out for my share. But she looked out the window as if she hadn't noticed, and I saw that she wasn't going to give me any of what she still had left.